To Remember With Tears

The island of Torrismore is moving towards its death. Each year the Scottish mainland claims more of its families, and more ambitious youngsters cross over the water into the twentieth century.

Cruachan Campbell's son Roddy is one of them: gone ostensibly to sell a watch and bring back flour and other necessities, but in fact gone for ever. Each week Cruachan expects his son's return—because he cannot conceive of leaving Torrismore himself. Other families may go, but not his.

What keeps Cruachan here, in a corrugated-iron shack which clangs and leaks in foul weather, scratching a living from the scanty soil? In a corner of the croft stands the half-finished new house he started to build more than thirty years ago. A weird mixture of castle and cathedral, it stands for Cruachan's faith in God and in a future no one around him can see.

In another writer's hands the story of the Campbells—the unhappy wife, the two problem girls, the old grandfather—might have been treated as unalloyed tragedy. But John Quigley makes of it a grim comedy, serious in its implications but irresistibly humorous in its treatment.

The author, whose first novel this is, has been a journalist on Scottish newspapers and now exports Scotch whisky.

John Quigley

To Remember
With Tears

HUTCHINSON OF LONDON

HUTCHINSON & CO. (*Publishers*) LTD
178–202 Great Portland Street, London, W.1

London Melbourne Sydney
Auckland Bombay Toronto
Johannesburg New York

★

First published 1963

© John Quigley 1963

*This book has been set in Bembo type face. It has
been printed in Great Britain by The Anchor Press,
Ltd., in Tiptree, Essex, on Antique Wove paper.*

I

SMALL green waves rippled on to the pebble shore as Cruachan Campbell sat on a rock by the Bay of the Angels and looked across the warm sea. It was so hot in the August sunshine that almost as soon as the water ran back down the beach the white pebbles were dry again. Cruachan did not notice how fast the sun dried the pebbles, nor did he hear the man trudging towards him along the stony track or see the big brown bird that flapped from the dark shadows of the hill above. What Cruachan was watching for was the thirty-foot, once-a-week motor-launch that linked the island with the Scottish mainland.

He was certain that when the boat reached the jetty at the other end of the big bay his son Roddy would be standing among the boxes and parcels of supplies.

It was nearly three months since Cruachan had called Roddy on to the grass outside the tin house where they lived and told him that he wanted him to go over on the next mail-boat and sell his good gold watch in Oban. Cruachan had bought the watch on a visit to the mainland many years before, in the days when he had been able to earn small but regular sums of money by ferrying goods and passengers between the island and the steamer that used to sail into the bay.

The watch was a cumbersome affair with a gold flap to protect the face, and although Cruachan had dropped it and stopped the ticking the very first day he had it, he had nevertheless worn it regularly ever since on Sundays. Every Sunday morning he lifted the watch from its brass hook beside the fireplace and rubbed it gently on his trouser leg till the gold case gleamed. After he had it shining properly he always shook it carefully a few times and held it to his ear to hear the tick for a few seconds until the damaged spring came to rest again. Although the hands had not moved for many years, Cruachan was always hopeful that some Sunday when he shook the watch the hidden mechanism would come miraculously to life.

The gold watch was the last possession of any value that Cruachan had left and only after long consideration had he finally decided to sell it to raise some money to help keep things going at the tin house until he and Roddy could build a lazybed and grow a good crop of potatoes.

Cruachan expected to get at least ten pounds for the watch, for he had heard that gold was fetching a good price these days, and when Roddy climbed into the boat for Oban he had taken with him a long list of articles to bring back.

Cruachan wanted to lay in a 110 lb. sack of flour, a big bag of oatmeal, a whole round of cheese, a side of bacon and some tins of pineapples, so that when the next winter storms isolated the island they would not be left without food. He had also instructed Roddy to bring home some clay pipes and some good-smelling tobacco with the remains of the money.

Roddy had hardly said a word to his father as they walked round the bay to the boat and if Cruachan had not been so excited at the prospect of having a good supply of food and tobacco in the house he might have wondered at the odd way his son glanced at him.

Although more than eighty days had passed since Roddy had sailed away, Cruachan still expected to see him back. Every day there was a mail-boat Cruachan hurried along to meet it, for he was always sure that this time Roddy would be on board with the articles he had sent him to buy.

6

Once a crofter from over the other side of the mountain had suggested that perhaps something had happened to the boy. Cruachan had become very angry. 'By Goddy,' he shouted at the man, 'I just does not know what all this impatience is for! Roddy's only been away since the other day. You would think he had been away for years, or something.'

This morning, as he sat with the smooth waves lapping at his rubber boots, Cruachan was certain that he would soon be stumbling back along the bay with a 110 lb. sack of flour on his back and Roddy behind, telling of the things he had seen in the big town. He turned and looked across the island, over the unworked and unworkable earth of his own land to the abandoned crofts and crumbling houses of the people who were gone. He could hear the waves running up on the pebbles and he could hear the pebbles clicking together as the waves ran back to the sea. For a moment his attention wandered.

Cruachan thought that tomorrow, maybe, he would get his spade and creel out and see if he could start gathering earth to build a lazybed of dry, airy soil on top of the waterlogged peat and rock. He remembered that he had decided the same thing two weeks ago and at various times during not only that year but every year, for as long back as he could recall. But suddenly, unreasonably, the endless hope that neither God nor man could ever quite kill began to rise in his heart.

It was the same every year. As he felt the heat in the ground and saw the heather budding and the bracken rising hard and shaggy on the hillside, Cruachan felt an urgent need to associate himself in some way with the island and the earth of which the island was made. But with only three inches of waterlogged peat and the rest rock there was nothing much he could do. He had not yet found the time to carry the earth for a lazybed, although he had been thinking seriously about it for almost forty years.

Cruachan had the thinly white and burning look of a man who

was hungry, but not for bread alone. The empty clay pipe at which he sucked, the broken stem clutched tightly between his gums, the cold bowl cradled forlornly in his hands, gave the last stroke of sadness to his face.

The place where he sat was littered like a scrapyard. There were two old armchairs, dozens of wooden boxes and cases, a rotting mattress, several broken farming implements, an iron bedstead and the rusting chassis of a perambulator which he used to pull his peats along the track from the bog.

The house itself was built of corrugated-iron sheeting and it had been rocked and shaken by the Atlantic winds for more than sixty years. The pitch-pine beams round which it was assembled were now splintered and rotten. The rusty bolts had snapped at various points, and since it had never occurred to Cruachan that they might be replaced, loose sections all round the house rattled in the smallest breeze and clanged deafeningly when the wind was strong.

Nothing about the house had been repaired or painted for more than thirty years, for Cruachan always said it was a waste of time and money when he was busy building a big brick house, anyway.

His new house stood about two hundred yards away on the other side of The Angels, the two great pillars of curiously shaped rock that gave the bay its name.

But although he had started building it thirty-three years before, he had not so far managed to get the roof on. At one end of the front wall a round turret stood about twenty feet high. This was the part of the big brick house that Cruachan liked best. It was the part of the house that he visualized as being God's. Cruachan was building the big brick house as much for God as for Flora and his children. All his life he had felt a need to honour God. This house was to be his personal monument to his creator.

From along the bay the house looked like a mixture of castle and cathedral, for on the back wall, opposite the turret, there was the

8

beginning of a spire which Cruachan planned eventually to be fifty feet high. The walls of the house were neither straight nor plumb and when Cruachan had been short of cement he had stuck the bricks together with mud.

The big brick house was his prayer in brick and mortar; preposterous, pathetic, incredible; a ramshackle symbol of the man himself.

Over his shoulder dry gorse crackled on the lower slopes of the mountain. He wondered when the rain would come. It had been dry for three days, but he knew it would not last.

He rose from the rock, wincing slightly as he straightened. At the same time the man who had been coming along the track swung himself over the dry-stone wall that surrounded the tin house. The man came over the wall carefully in case it fell down. Much of it had already collapsed, and it lay where it fell, although Cruachan was always meaning to do something about it.

The man looked about. It had been like this for as long as he could remember, although the last time he had been at the house, about a year before, Cruachan had been talking about cleaning it all up. Something must have intervened.

' 'Morning, Cruachan,' he called. 'Enjoying the sun?'

Cruachan looked at the long manila envelope the man was carrying. 'Good morning to you, Sandy McCaskill,' he said. He knew what was in the envelope and he hated it. He started to edge away. 'In you go, Sandy, away into the house and have a cup of tea with Flora. I'm just hurrying away to meet the mail-boat. Something tells me Roddy will be on it this day for sure.'

McCaskill looked out to sea with the far-seeing eye of an old sailor. 'Plenty of time, Cruachan,' he said. 'Plenty of time for you to make your mark on this petition I've got here, after me leaving the post office unattended just to get your name down.'

9

Although the population of the island was only a few score, he spoke as if there might be an angry crowd waiting for stamps when he got back. He pushed open the door of the tin house, stepped over the sagging step and went in.

Cruachan followed. 'I'll come in for a minute,' he said, 'but I'm not for signing.'

McCaskill was used to austerity but the inside of the tin house always made him feel like a millionaire. In the hearth there was a peat fire and in front of it a plain wooden table with a few chairs wedged under it. Near the fire there was a bed and behind it a dresser. There was no other furniture in the room, nor were there carpets or curtains. And there was no ceiling.

The walls extended upwards until they disappeared into the shadowy roof space. The flaking, corrugated sections which formed the roof and the rotting beams on which they sat were all visible. From one beam an oil lamp with a cracked and sooty glass funnel hung down into the centre of the room. There was only one window with glass in it. The others were boarded over with wood.

Sitting at the side of the fire was Cruachan's younger daughter Mairi Fiona. She had been peeling potatoes into a chipped enamel basin with numb disinterest, but when the men came in she began to work as fast as the blunt blade would let her.

Cruachan kicked the toe of his boot against a leg of the table. His brow was sullen.

'By Goddy, Sandy, the dear Lord knows I has told ye a countless times I's uninterested in that bally petition of yours,' he said. 'Nobody here at the tin house wants moved off this old island.'

McCaskill shook the envelope he carried. 'Nobody but you is thinking of this island of Torrismore as a fit place to live these days, Cruachan,' he said.

'With the lobsters and the fish all gone and nobody able to grow

10

anything worth having out the earth, the only thing left for them to do is blow this island right up into the sky before things get any worse. Believe me, one o' these days them Government men from Edinburgh is going to load us all into a boat and sail us off somewhere else where a man can make enough to live on.'

All his life Cruachan had loved the island, and although it had never given him back anything but hardship and sorrow, he could not bear to hear what McCaskill was saying about it. He bent down and lifted a peat from the hearth and waved it in the face of his visitor. 'Man, man, Sandy,' he said, 'what you don't know when you stand there raving is that this island and this peat and me is all the same stuff. I'd feel like a wee white lamb being snatched from under its mother if I had to leave this old tin-house croft. The dear Lord set me down on this island like He did the heather and the mountain up there, and when the time comes for Him to lift me up again this is where I'll be.'

He sighed ferociously and waved through the dirty window to the derelict fields beyond. 'This is my home town,' he said passionately. 'This is where I lives. Them towns over the water there is not for me, or all them bally roads and houses, either.'

McCaskill looked away. 'Just the same, Cruachan, looks like maybe they mean to take us off the island right soon. Them officials was here last month counting the sheep and the cattle and asking me a wheen o' questions.'

Cruachan spat into the fire.

'When I hears you talk like that, Sandy McCaskill, and then I looks out there and sees the holy sun shining over the hill and when I feels the breeze coming over the island smelling all sweet and gentle from the peat smoke and the bog myrtle, then I think you and me must be different kinds of men, and the dear Lord knows which He likes best.'

McCaskill slapped his forehead. It was a scene they had acted together so many times. 'For God's sake, man, don't be so damned stupid! If the rest of us leave you'll have to come as well.'

Mairi Fiona after peeling every second or third potato was looking at herself in a hand mirror and giving her long black hair a pat, a twist or some other adjustment. McCaskill pointed to her. 'What about your family?' he said. 'Don't you care what happens to Mairi Fiona and Our Sheena and Flora?'

'No, he doesna give a damn what happens to anybody as long as he gets sittin' out there against the wall mumping away about the great things he's goin' to do once he gets the energy to get started.'

It was Flora. She had come like a bat from the shadows of the kitchen.

Mairi Fiona giggled. 'Sure they're always arguing like this, Mammy?'

Flora turned on her. 'Get on wi' they potatoes, you silly wee bitch,' she said. 'There's naebody talking to you.'

The ragged skirt that Flora wore had been made from a potato sack. Above it there was the top half of a dress that she had salvaged when the bottom bit became too tattered to wear. The buttons were all missing and it was held shut by safety-pins. Hanging round her shoulders and fastened in front by another safety-pin was a black shawl. Flora wore the shawl because she did not have a coat and her thin blood was for ever cold, even inside the house.

Cruachan pulled his blue fisherman's jersey down very deliberately and looked at Flora as if she were vermin.

'Sandy and me is discussing something in private,' he said. 'The dear Lord knows we don't need you at all.'

Flora cackled as she went back to the kitchen. 'You an' the dear Lord make me sick,' she said.

McCaskill had been turned away, reading a tract that hung from a bolt-head on the wall: *My God Shall Supply All Thy Need.* He wondered when the supplies would come. He stepped forward.

'Now come on, sign this petition like a reasonable man, Cruachan. The last one had every name on it but you Campbells'.'

Cruachan gestured at the paper that McCaskill had taken from the envelope. 'Man, Sandy, ye should've left that precious document in that wee post office of yours. Ye shouldn't have tired yourself out travelling away over here, now, for by Goddy I'm not for signing and never will.'

Suddenly Cruachan laughed. 'I tell you what, Sandy. Here's a bargain made before the witness o' the dear Lord. I'll leave this island when the birds peck holes in the rocks or the sea stops moving or those pebbles out there turn to gold. Just when you see any of these things, Sandy, you tell me and I'll do my signing on that bit o' paper.'

He was still laughing as he went out the door, stepped over a low section of the wall and hurried along the track.

When the mail-boat sailed in Cruachan splashed out as far as his rubber boots would let him. When he saw that Roddy was not there the expression on his face hardly changed.

He caught hold of the side of the boat and shouted: 'See any sign of Roddy when you was over the water there?'

The passengers shook their heads and looked away. There was nothing they could say.

'I consider Roddy has just met up with something that's taking up his time a while,' Cruachan said. 'I'm expecting him back any day now. Once Roddy gets back things is going to be a whole heap brighter along at the tin house. Roddy and me is going to carry enough earth to make the biggest bally lazybed this old island has ever seen.'

No one living understood better than Cruachan how a man could be delayed. He had been delayed in everything he had ever tried to do. He had been delayed in building his new brick house, in making a lazybed, in marrying Flora. He had been delayed continually every day of his life. But Cruachan knew that although they had been going on for a long time these delays were only temporary and that nothing could stop a man for ever. He believed with all his heart that Roddy had been delayed in some similar manner to himself, but that practically any time now he would be back and they would start work together on a lazybed.

2

IT WAS evening when Cruachan arrived back at the tin house. The sun had gone and the rain had come and above the mountain the sky was black like Easdale slate.

Mairi Fiona sat on the floor, her legs and feet drawn under her skirt, her back supported against a packing-case that stood at the side of the fire, her body shaking with laughter. When she saw her father she threw up her hands as if to welcome him to the merriment. Then she pointed to the bed. There was another girl lying on it and Flora was bending over her.

'Our Sheena's making the funniest noises you ever heard, Daddy!' Mairi Fiona screamed.

'Shut your blethering mouth, you stupid wee fool!' Cruachan shouted at her. He rushed like a startled rabbit into the centre of the room.

In the glow of the fire the room, so bleak by day, looked almost fit to be lived in, almost part of a home.

The girl in the bed was Our Sheena, Cruachan's other daughter, and she was twisting painfully under the thin, patched sheets which had been stitched together from flour bags. Her cheeks were gaunt and red and when she opened her eyes they glistened brightly.

Flora stood over her with what might have been an expression of motherly anxiety. With one hand she was trying to lift Our Sheena's head from the mattress—for there was no pillow—and with the other she was holding out a cup filled with water. For an instant it looked as if she were behaving like a real woman, as if, for a time, the dark angel were not weeping in her ear. But what might have been concern was only alarm—a selfish substitute.

'Here, drink this nice cold water now an' for pity's sake stop that terrible noise.' There was a sob of panic in Flora's mainland voice, so flat compared to the island lilt.

Our Sheena brushed the cup away, and then, clutching at her stomach, began softly to moan.

'Tell your mother what's wrong with ye, Our Sheena,' Flora wailed. 'Ye're frightening the heart out o' me with this carry-on.'

Cruachan stood by the lamp, puzzled and resentful at this unexpected upset. He was hungry. Although he had visited several crofters on the way home, no one had offered him food.

'By hell, if I leave this bally tin house for just ten minutes you all get up to some trouble or other.' It was a snarl without ferocity or force. He moved nearer the bed and peered down at his daughter.

'When did ye get back, Our Sheena? What's wrong with you? Have ye hurt yourself?'

The girl on the bed made no reply, but Mairi Fiona's voice came eagerly across the room.

'Our Sheena must be dying,' she said. 'Anybody in all that suffering must be dying, all right.'

Only one occupant of the room shouldered Our Sheena's affliction with indifference. Grampa Campbell was perched on a chair by the fire, stoically ruminating on the advantages of death over life and, more immediately, on the possibility of coaxing a little bread or cheese out of Flora.

It was no sudden depression or the sight of the sick girl that had turned the old man's mind to death. For years Grampa Campbell had been thinking of little else. His coffin, made from some lengths of oak wood that he had found on the beach, lay ready beside his bed in the back room.

It was a constant source of annoyance to him that he was still alive. He knew that Cruachan and Flora hated him and would have forgotten him in a day if he walked out of the tin house and never came back.

'I just can't work out why the dear Lord does not fix me up so I can get in this box and stay there,' Grampa would sometimes say, as he sat polishing the smooth wood of his coffin. 'The Lord is not playing it fair with me now that I'm all kitted up and ready to go.'

'By Hell, the Lord never did mean people to go making their own coffins!' Cruachan always told him angrily. 'I consider you are annoying the dear Lord so bad with that bally coffin He is keeping you alive for spite so you just cannot get using it.'

Now, as Grampa listened to the noises Our Sheena was making, he wondered enviously if she were dying.

Flora drank the water that our Sheena had refused.

'One minute she wasna here and the next she was,' she said, glowering at the girl. 'Mairi Fiona and me were busy working in the kitchen when the door banged open and there was this moaning and groaning. Our Sheena was lying in bed, as large as life, still wi' all her clothes on and her bible just dinged doon there in the corner.'

A grey bonnet lay on the floor beside the bible. It was the trade mark of the order to which Our Sheena belonged—the Assembly with God as Father and the Holy Scriptures as Law.

The girl's outstanding appearance was obvious even as she lay in bed. She was six feet four inches tall and her feet hung over the end of the mattress, clear of the bedclothes. She was now twenty-five years old and she had been a missionary for nearly three years.

It was Abrach Morrison, a veteran evangelist of the islands, who had persuaded Cruachan to allow her to attend the Assembly's study course at its headquarters in Edinburgh. Cruachan, although he detested the thought of the mainland, had agreed because he felt that God might gaze less harshly on his sins if he had a preacher in the family. He also saw in the suggestion the opportunity of laying down the burden of nourishing Our Sheena's gigantic body.

The girl had gone to Edinburgh and spent six months on a course designed to acquaint her, theoretically, with the intricacies of sin and the wickedness of Man. But Our Sheena—by doing what came naturally to her—rapidly achieved a deeper insight into sin than her tutors had planned.

The Assembly with God as Father and the Holy Scriptures as Law was based on a literal acceptance of every word in the Bible and it regarded the experiencing of any pleasure on the Sabbath as the vilest sin of all.

At the end of her indoctrination Our Sheena had sworn an oath renouncing books, tobacco, films, alcohol, jewellery and cosmetics. She had then been sent back to her watery world of damp mist and wet rock, equipped with a bible, an armful of tracts and a heart full of love for God—and Man. Now there was hardly an island in the whole of the Hebrides in which she was not known.

The island women did not approve of the way Our Sheena's bright fair hair hung down to her waist, and they did not like her way of saving male sinners, which they thought put too much emphasis on sisterly love. In countless Hebridean gossip groups she was known as Sister Jezebel.

There was something about the girl's great size that filled men with fascinated ambition. It was an invitation to destruction, yet in the pondering of its enormous mysteries some men believed they had found God. In its holy embrace many male sins had been forgiven, or so Our Sheena had promised. Despite the scandalized or salacious sniggers that her appearance, her performance or her trespasses provoked, Our Sheena soldiered diligently on for the Lord in the rock-firm belief that Sabbath-breakers were an abomination and that men needed more than spiritual comfort.

Her hair was stringy with sweat as she twisted in the bed, but even in pain she had the hard attraction of a carving created in some

18

previous age and excavated in a remote corner of the earth. As Cruachan looked down at her he did not feel that she was his. She seemed to belong more to the primitive world of the angels outside, and he viewed her as he would have a public monument that required cleaning or some other attention.

As he watched, Our Sheena spoke.

'Get Dr Munro, Daddy,' she said. 'This pain the dear Lord has sent me is as cruel as the devil himself. It's jagging at my stomach like the fires of hell.'

'Aye, get the doctor quick instead of standing there gawking like an old gander,' Flora said.

Cruachan looked alarmed.

'Looks to me like Our Sheena will be all right without any doctor,' he said, moving quickly to the fire and standing with his back to it. 'It's just a sudden attack like I sometimes get myself, that's all it is. The dear Lord will have Our Sheena fine in a minute or two without any bally doctor.'

He took his empty pipe from his pocket and started working on it with the concentration of a praying monk. He blew through it desperately and then tapped it on the hearth as if the reason for its cold lifelessness was a hidden blockage and not the absence of tobacco.

When he was finished he put the pipe away again and peered through the shadows of the room with huge intensity. 'Our Sheena's looking better already, so she is,' he said.

Almost immediately the girl started moaning.

'Get away an' fetch Dr. Munro, ye lazy old stick,' Flora shouted.

The doctor lived on Linga, a wooded, more fertile island, separated from Torrismore by a two-mile-wide strait of water which swirled over an area of submerged rocks known as the Beast of Torrismore.

He was summoned to urgent cases on Torrismore, which had no telephone, by the lighting of an oil-soaked bonfire which stood in perpetual readiness on a small headland at the narrowest part of the channel. The headland was on the south side of the island, two miles away from the tin house. It would be a long, wet walk, but Cruachan knew defeat when he saw it. It had accompanied him with remorseless attention throughout his life.

'Just let me have a bite to eat an' I'll away, then,' he muttered.

At the mention of food Grampa began to stir with sluggish life, like an amoeba. 'I'll have a bite with you, son, just not to have ye eating on your lone,' he quavered. His lips moved in anticipation, like a laboratory specimen demonstrating a conditioned reflex. A bit of bread or cheese. Anything would do. It helped him to sleep if he had something in his stomach, which was not often.

He started to rise hopefully, but Cruachan, who was walking to the kitchen with the expression of a man committed to some solemn self-sacrifice, pushed him to the chair again with a negligent, almost absent-minded action. He had almost reached the kitchen when Flora scuttled past him.

'Will ye talk of food when Our Sheena's dying of pain?' she asked. 'Ye'll eat nothing till ye get Dr. Munro back here and see what's wrong with the girl. It might be her appendix. She'll maybe need an operation.'

Mairi Fiona giggled. 'There's never been an operation in here before, has there, Daddy?' she said.

Flora spun round on her, the tackety soles of her boots tearing splinters out of the floorboards.

'Haud your wheesht, girl, and not be keeping your father back wi' your silly mumping when your sister's driving me out o' my head.'

Flora's anxiety to get the doctor was based largely on a wish to make Cruachan exert himself and only fractionally on solicitude for the girl in the bed.

'The dear Lord seems determined to make my time on this earth nothing but misery and want,' Cruachan whimpered. 'Even in my own home I can't get either rest or food.'

20

He was almost weeping when he went out.

It was dark now, with only a quarter-moon behind the clouds, and he slid continually on long tendrils of seaweed or stumbled over stones which stuck out of the path. This was the island's highway. There was no road or any other surfaced way on which a wheeled vehicle could run.

On one side the sea gurgled its endless message to the rocks and on the other side boulder-strewn turf undulated to the foot of the high ground. There were no inhabited houses now on this side of the island, only ruins round which bats swooped and in the gritty depths of which small night creatures scuffled for survival on the same melancholy treadmill as the islanders.

It took Cruachan almost an hour to reach the bonfire.

The oily rags which were bundled round the base flamed into life with the first match. Soon the whole structure—boxes, driftwood, fence-posts, old clothes—went up in a burst of fire that crackled and rumbled with such force that Cruachan had to move away. The heat cheered him, although he knew that he would now have to wait in the rain for more than an hour before there was any hope of the doctor's boat chugging in to the crumbling concrete jetty.

3

THE sound of the old wire-operated bell jangled down the corridors of the big house and into the study to where Dr. Thomas Munro sat. His feet were stretched out towards the glowing peats and he was reaching for the cigar-box that lay on a low table beside his chair.

He heard the front door being opened, voices meeting, and then the approaching footsteps of Mary McCallum, his housekeeper. He made a quick diagnosis of the situation and sighed. The prognosis was not hopeful. He left the cigar-box untouched.

The door opened and Mary's round, vexed face appeared. 'It's an absolute terrible shame when you're sitting there so nice by the fire, Doctor, and at this time of night, too, after such a long day,' she said.

The doctor glanced wistfully at his cigar-box as he waited for her to go on.

His remoteness from the centres of sophistication had never been allowed to interfere with the mild indulgences that he had enjoyed in the days of his magnificence. He still had dinner at eight, when he could manage it, with a glass of dry sherry served in the drawing-room beforehand, and a cigar and a glass of brandy in front of the peat fire in his study after it.

'It was Calum at the door to say the beacon was burning over on Torrismore,' Mary said. 'He says it must have been blazing away for a good long while before anybody saw it, for it's gone out now, and the whole place black again.'

The doctor drew his feet away from the fire. 'Tell Calum to get the boat ready,' he said. 'I'll be down in a minute.'

Dr. Thomas Munro was now a man more than seventy years old, but he travelled the archipelago of four small islands over which his practice was scattered with all the vigour of his boyhood and the devotion of a saint. He had fled to the islands from a rich middle-class practice in the West End of Glasgow, driven by a need for something that he could not find among the neurotic women and fat business men who filled his purse and at the same time robbed his life of the sense of purpose which he craved.

He was already past forty when, to the astonishment of the islanders, he had stepped carefully ashore on Torrismore, wearing a tile hat, striped trousers and an exquisite frock-coat created for him by a Bath Street tailor for a sum of money that would have kept any of the islanders for a year.

While Mary called the boatman, the doctor pulled on heavy seaboots and an oilskin. An hour later he stepped lightly ashore on the jetty at Torrismore. The rucksack in which he carried his dispensary rested easily on his slim back. In one hand he held his bag and in the other an old lantern.

'Well, Cruachan, you need me?'

It was the greeting that he had been giving since he started in the islands, and although he must have said it a hundred thousand times, it still came out of the long, serene face with fresh simplicity. Cruachan always thought it was the very thing that God Himself might say if He appeared in response to a man's prayers.

'It's Our Sheena, Doctor,' he said, gripping the old man's arm. 'She's sick. The lass is lying in bed rolling about like the devil was at her and making noises enough to send the boulders rattling down the mountain with fright.'

When they reached the tin house Our Sheena was quiet, but the fever still burned in her eyes.

Dr. Munro put down his bag and swung the rucksack off his back. 'Boil some water, please, Mrs. Campbell,' he said. Hot water, used in a dozen different ways, was one of the principal weapons in his old-fashioned pharmacopoeia, but it was also a scarce commodity in the primitive island houses and a good supply of it was one of the first things he always asked for.

When he had taken off his sou'wester and oilskin he went over to Our Sheena. He had been present at the girl's birth and he marvelled every time he saw how big she had grown.

'Well, girlie, this is a fine way to come home,' he said, taking her wrist. 'Where's the pain?'

Our Sheena turned over on to her side and through the fever and strain there had come into her eyes an expression that might have been either embarrassment or apprehension.

'It's my stomach, Doctor,' she said in a low voice. 'There's a terrible pain in it. It's been coming on me for days, but I kept on working for the Lord as long as I could.'

'Aye! Very thoughtful indeed.' He let go of her wrist and put his watch away.

'It got so bad this morning when I was over in Orasay that I had to jump up from where I was praying and come home to the tin house. I was lucky there was a boat coming over.'

Dr. Munro listened with amused compassion moving over his smooth brown face.

'Well, let's have a look, then, and we'll soon see what it's all about. Just let me see where the pain is.'

Our Sheena cast a look of alarm in the direction of the family group at the fireplace. She made no attempt to move the mat that covered her.

The doctor unwound his stethoscope and draped it round his neck. A small wind was shaking a delicate ripple of metallic sound from the loose sections of the house.

'What's keeping you, girl?' he said. Then: 'Never heed them over there. They're not bothering about us. Just let me see this tummy that's causing all the bother.'

Our Sheena shut her eyes and pushed down the bed-mat. She was still fully dressed.

Cruachan, Flora and Mairi Fiona sat staring into the fire. Grampa had gone to bed in the other room. Apart from the house itself, the only sound came from the low questions and answers that passed between the girl and the doctor.

At last the old man moved away from the bed and began to wash his hands with great attention in the chipped enamel basin that Flora had placed on the table and filled with hot water from a black iron kettle that hung from a cleek above the peats. He did not look at the faces that were watching him. Nor did he speak. After almost a minute of silence Cruachan could wait no longer.

'Well, Doctor, what's wrong wi' Our Sheena?' His voice was almost petulant. 'You're frightening us all just standing there saying nothing at all after taking all that time to look at her.'

The doctor smiled. 'Oh, there's nothing to be frightened about, Cruachan,' he said. 'Our Sheena will be right as rain in a day or two. Just keep her warm in bed and if necessary I'll come back and have another look at her.'

'Is she not sick at all, then?' Flora's voice, if its flatness could be said to have any expression, seemed to be tinged with resentment.

'Oh, yes. She's sick all right. The poor child's got a bad chill in her stomach. If she'd done something about it sooner she'd never have been in this state.'

He put away his stethoscope and clicked his bag shut. Then he looked suddenly upwards at the gently palpitating roof and coughed with unnatural violence. Our Sheena was watching him with bright eyes, as if waiting.

'As a matter of fact, though, there's something else as well,' he said, still looking at the roof. 'Heaven knows why I should be the one to tell you, but Our Sheena's asked me to.' Again he stopped.

'By Goddy, Doctor, tell us and be done with it, then!' Cruachan shouted, scuffling his feet on the floorboards. 'Her mammy and me is brave enough to bear any news the dear Lord sends to us.'

Dr. Munro swung on him, angered by his tone, irritated by his own hesitance, annoyed that although he had been faced with the same situation many times, he always found himself incapable of dealing with it in clinical calm.

'Man, man, where are your eyes? Do you not know an expectant mother when you see one?' he snapped. 'This lass of yours is big enough with bairn for anybody to see it.'

Flora was the first to recover.

'Bairn?' she muttered. 'But we never saw Our Sheena at all, Doctor. She just ran in when there was none o' us here.'

She seemed more concerned with the doctor's astonishment at their blindness than with the situation he had revealed.

Then: 'But Our Sheena canna be having a baby, Doctor. She's not married.'

The doctor threw the towel on the table and started to pull down his sleeves. 'That's never stopped anybody having a baby—unfortunately. God knows our Sheena's having a baby all right, I can tell you, so mind you keep her fine and warm in bed. The chill she has is simple enough, but we don't want it starting any complications.'

Mairi Fiona's eyes turned demurely to the floor.

'Sure this is terrible, Mammy,' she said with a cunning sideways glance at Flora. 'Our Sheena's not supposed to have a baby when she's not married, and her a missionary too.'

The child giggled as some profane picture sped across her mind.

Cruachan was shaking his head slowly.

'So Our Sheena's having a baby,' he said softly, as if conversing with someone standing very near, but invisible. 'I just does not understand it at all. It seems to be a thing that keeps happening to these lady missionaries. It just does not seem like the work of the dear Lord to me, at all.'

He went to the fire, and, crouching down in front of it, absent-mindedly held the glowing end of a peat to his empty pipe and sucked strongly at it till it burned his tongue.

The doctor began to pull on his oilskin. It was a long way home, but he might yet have time for a glass of brandy at the fire before going to bed. He went over to the girl.

'If you keep yourself nice and snug and sip the hot water your mother will give you you'll be rid of that chill by the end of the week.' He smiled reprovingly at her. 'But I'm afraid it will be the end of the year before you get any relief from the other thing.'

Our Sheena did not answer. She had turned on her side and pulled up her long legs. She looked, in the glow of the gently swaying lamp, like a large wild flower of some unknown but heroic strain. Her pain had been soothed by the doctor's assurances, the weight of her secret lightened by its telling. She was settling into the deep, dreamless rest of someone very young and innocent.

4

FOR nine days it had been raining. The peat had passed the limits of its almost infinite capacity to hold the rain and the water now lay on top of the overburdened land. Whenever Cruachan walked across the croft his feet sank and the ground made piteous noises. But the harsh drops continued to fall from the August sky—viciously ensuring that where there was no drainage nothing would ever grow; spitefully flattening what the earth had laboured to produce in those rare places where men had painfully created small patches of fertility.

Normally, spring drifted over as dry and gentle as a moth, luring on the men who still had heart enough left to plant the land. Then, when the seeds were in, the rains came, flooding the fields and rotting the plants. From the resonant roof and walls of the tin house the rain struck a noise that would have stunned any ordinary person but to which the Campbells, by some swift evolutionary process, had grown impervious.

Cruachan's clothes were moist and mildewed as he manœuvred his chilled limbs into them at dawn on the morning of the ninth day. He groaned at the physical and mental effort involved.

The previous night Flora had heard that a man was needed for the laying of a new path in the grounds of Finnoch Castle which stood on a rocky outcrop separated from Torrismore by a sandy ford. The castle was owned by an Englishman and was inhabited throughout most of the year only by a factor and his wife.

Such opportunities for earning money were rare in Torrismore and Flora had urged and threatened Cruachan so eloquently that he had not only agreed to apply for the job but had actually gone to sleep convinced that the idea was his.

When he left the house only the lower slopes of the mountain were visible through the shrouding rain. After an hour of lonely walking he saw movement ahead of him. Outside a thatch-roofed house at the side of the track a man was lifting peats from an untidy stack and placing them in a pail for carrying indoors. It was McIsaac.

When Cruachan saw who it was he left the track to avoid him, but McIsaac was not to be disregarded. He put down his pail and stepped over the squelching peat with almost ludicrous haste.

'Is that you yourself, Cruachan?' he called out. 'Well, well, it is true a man never knows what he will see in the bracken when he goes out to get a few wee bits o' peat for his fire, and at this uncivilized hour o' the morning, too, and you a man that likes his bed so much, as the whole island o' Torrismore knows so well.'

Cruachan kept his head lowered and pushed on as if he had not seen or heard anything. But McIsaac only called out again in an even louder voice and from a greatly decreased range.

'Don't be passing me by like that, now, Cruachan Campbell, and me never seeing you for such a big while and us cousins as well, just a few times removed.'

The voice was so close that Cruachan could no longer pretend that he had not heard. He stopped and waited for the man to come through the saturated grass and bracken.

'Is everything all right over at the tin house?' McIsaac asked. He had a crafty expression that was intended to suggest concern. 'Nothing wrong with Flora or any of the family, I hope?'

Cruachan's voice was stiff.

29

'Everybody over at the tin house is fine,' he said.

The rain was running down McIsaac's bald head like drops of mercury.

'Maybe it is Roddy, then, that brings you away over here in all this rain. Maybe it is you have heard Roddy is over this way someplace?' The annoying voice had dropped to a whisper that assumed some sort of mutual understanding of Roddy's whereabouts. It was a suggestion that Cruachan could not accept in silence.

'By Hell,' he exclaimed, 'every man on this island knows damn' well Roddy went over to Oban last week to do some business I needed done! What would I be needing to look up here for Roddy for, then?'

He tried to push past, but McIsaac gripped him by the sleeve.

'What for would you be wandering so far from the tin house in such a weather for, then, Cruachan? Where are you going, then, if it is not for Roddy?'

It was a direct question and Cruachan's nature was such that he could not help giving a direct answer.

'I am going to look for some work at Finnoch Castle,' he said, 'and the dear Lord knows I am in a big hurry. Flora would not want me to be late.'

With angry strength he pushed the man out of his way and walked on.

Blair, the factor, was still at his nine o'clock breakfast when Cruachan arrived at his house, dripping but eager. Mrs. Blair took his cap and jacket for drying, then showed him into a dull room where the factor himself looked at him over his breakfast plate with wary amiability. He was a mainland Scot recently imported to the island by his master. Like all his kind, he was underpaid but welcome to any perquisites that his ingenuity enabled him to extract from the tight budget on which the estate was run.

Cruachan sniffed at the rousing fragrance of the fried bread and eggs which lay heaped on the factor's plate. Blair continued to cut vigorously at the food as he nodded Cruachan to a black horse-hair sofa.

'Well, well, man,' he said in a voice distorted by his breakfast, but affable enough, 'is the island sinking wi' all this rain to bring ye running here at this hour o' the morning?'

'Oh, there is rain enough for it, all right, but it is not that, Mr. Blair,' Cruachan said with a shy laugh. 'It is some work I have come to see you about. Some woman told my wife that you was looking for a man to make a new path up by the castle.'

The factor impaled half an egg and a crisp section of bread on his fork and pushed them into his mouth. Although he appeared to be concentrating on the food, he had not missed Cruachan's eagerness.

'My, my, it seems you islanders know what I'm wanting before I know it myself,' he said. 'It must be true, right enough, that ye all have the second sight.'

The big mahogany furniture, the floral wallpaper and the rows of gilt-framed pictures had made Cruachan nervous after the frugality of the tin house. Now the man's manner was worrying him.

'It was a woman told my wife you were wanting a man for a new path, Mr. Blair,' he said, rubbing the palms of his hands on his wet knees. 'Is it not right?'

'Oh, it's maybe true enough, but what would an auld man like you be wanting to make paths for? Would ye not be better sitting comfy in front o' your fire enjoying your retirement?' He took his cup and gulped it empty with a noise like a man swilling out a coal-shed.

Cruachan saw the taunt, but his mind was too slow to provide him with a reply of the same kind.

'I'm not retired, Mr. Blair,' he said, 'and I'm not all that old neither. I can work like any other man. The trouble out here on Torrismore is getting some work to do. Flora heard you needed a man out here to make a new path up at the castle and I thought maybe you would give me the work. Flora got me up at the first blink o' light so that I'd be the first man here. There is hardly any food in the tin house except some meal at the bottom of the sack and a potato or two. I need any work that is going about.'

The factor had been listening to Cruachan's increasing nervousness with a broken smile on his face. He lifted the brown earthenware teapot from the nest of hand-knitted wool and refilled his cup.

'Oh, times are hard, right enough, as you say,' he sighed. 'Hard for all o' us, ye understand, Mr. Campbell. It's a real job I have here sometimes keeping this estate up to the mark. Things get run down and maybe we could be doing wi' a new path now that ye mention it.'

He stirred his tea and tested some from the spoon. Cruachan waited, his clothes becoming colder on his stiff body and the furnishings of the room growing more unfriendly.

'How much would ye be asking for a job like that, just supposing I decided to have it done?' Blair put his spoon down softly on the saucer as if the discussion had now reached a stage so sacred that any noise would have been irreverent.

Cruachan hardly hesitated. 'One pound a day.'

'Mr. Blair,' he said. 'That is the rate a man gets for a whole day's work.'

The factor frowned and bunched his eyebrows together. This was a part he had played in countless bargaining sessions and he knew all the moves.

'Man, man, ye value yerself high and no mistake about it,' he said with a sarcastic frown. 'A pound a day, ye say? Indeed, that's a kind of specialist's fee, I'm thinking. Ye maun be a right braw pathmaker and that's a fact.'

He laughed, shaking in his chair so that his teacup rattled in the saucer. Then he seized a slice of bread and ran it carefully round his plate in circles, soaking up the grease.

'But that is what a man gets for a day's work, Mr. Blair,' Cruachan protested. 'Any man that works all day gets a pound and the dear Lord knows that. Ask anybody, they'll tell you that's true, all right.'

'But, man, that's money for skilled work,' Blair said, banging the table. He knew that what Cruachan said was true, but he also knew that every penny he could retain on the job would stick to his own fingers. He had no disregard for Cruachan. It was a matter of impersonal economics. Justice did not arise, only avarice.

'Aye, for skilled work that kind o' money is,' he repeated, as if scandalized. 'And by a young fellow wi' good wind, at that, no' an auld man.'

Cruachan shook his head. 'But a pound is what a man gets, Mr. Blair.'

'Man, it's no' a civil engineer ye are, it's a navvy. Path-making is just for navvies. Sixteen-and-six a day is what I can pay for the work I need and not a ha'penny more.'

Cruachan sat like a beggar on the sofa. He did not know how it would be done, but he knew that the disputed money would come out of the estate coffers and be diverted into the factor's pocket.

Blair was saying: 'Don't look so glum, man, I'm not the one to hold it against ye for trying to make an extra bawbee. Ye're the first here and though your bones look gey rickety ye can have the job if ye like—starting the morn's morning, for I havena the time the day to show ye what's wanting. Sixteen-and-six a day and my missus 'll have a bowl o' broth for ye.'

Cruachan wanted to refuse, but he knew that behind him, somewhere through the smoky rain, there were men who would grasp at the work at the factor's price.

He hung his head and scuffed one boot on the floor.

'Very well, Mr. Blair,' he said. 'Sixteen shillings and sixpence a day, but I don't know what I'll tell Flora. Flora knows, all right, that the usual money a man gets for working all day is one pound.'

Blair poured the remains of the tea, holding the pot high and admiring the splashing noises made by the brown cataract as it fell into his cup. The pleasurable tightness of his breakfast against his waistband and the warm satisfaction radiating from his easy victory had put a new shine on the morning for him.

'Tell her there's a wheen o' places in the world where a man would kiss yer backside to work for half o' that—aye, and a quarter o't,' he said with a crude laugh. 'There's worse places nor Torrismore, ye know. Hong Kong, now. There's a place where the coolies slave all week for a bowl o' rice. Sixteen-and-six a day to them an' they'd be in Heaven, or wherever it is heathens go to.'

For an instant he had a vision of how rich he would grow if the economy of Torrismore could be equalized with that of Hong Kong and the islanders paid, if not in rice, then with oatmeal. Life, he thought, as he rose from the table, was a struggle. Aye, a struggle— and a bitter one. Ye had to be hard or it beat you. That was his trouble. He wasna half dour enough.

So changeable was Cruachan's nature that next morning when he left the tin house he turned his face up to the rain and stood for a few moments as if in sunshine. For some weeks, perhaps even months, he would have an assured income, however small. Not only would this buy food, it might stop Flora nagging so much.

Even better, he had concocted in his mind a belief that there would be a surplus which he would save until he had enough money to start work on the big brick house again.

He crossed the glistening wet grass to where the weird cathedral of his dreams stood broken and pitiful under the dark sky. He placed a reverent hand against the brickwork and felt the strange energy that lay there. Over the rough, improbable walls his hands roamed, testing the tenacity of the impoverished mortar, brushing from the innumerable ledges and crevices the blemishing deposits of crumbling masonry and creeping vegetation. He flexed his crackling knees, closed one adoring eye and squinted along a wall, miraculously debarring from his mind the grotesque imperfections. He saw only that another two or three courses of brick would complete it to the lax and ludicrous standard that he had set three decades before.

Astonishingly, the fervour that was in him then still burned, flickering sometimes but never expiring, tended, it seemed, by an unseen hand. Along with his love of the land it was the only constant factor in his nature.

He tingled with anticipation at the thought that soon, through the work he had found, he would be able to build the house higher. In his mind he saw it rising, one firm brick mounting on top of another, the disfiguring gaps disappearing under the artistry of his darting trowel, the rich and trusty cement setting in the sun until, at last, the walls stood hard and true and the wide vault of the roof closed over with wonderful precision. So real was the vision that a cry of adoration burst from his lips. It was like a prayer drifting up to the wet sky. For a moment longer he stood, then turned elatedly away.

The island, as on the previous morning, was deserted and soundless except for the low voice of the rain and the swishing of his feet through the bracken. As he approached the borders of McIsaac's croft he left the track, determined not to expose himself to another dose of the man's prying.

Because of the time that he had spent at the big brick house it was almost eight-fifteen when he arrived at the castle.

As he approached the factor's house for his instructions he heard a creaking sound. It was the noise of a barrow wheel revolving on an ungreased axle. It came from beyond a shrubbery that stood between the house and the castle. Like an animal smelling fire, Cruachan sensed trouble.

He stepped into the shrubbery and pushed his way through the dripping branches. When he reached the other side he saw the bent

35

figure of a man tumbling a load of broken rock from a barrow. It was McIsaac. And the rock that he had been wheeling was clearly bottoming for a new path. Even to a man with a mind as sluggish and trusting as his it was obvious to Cruachan that McIsaac was doing his job. He almost ran from the bushes. He wanted to burst out on the man and stone him with the rocks that lay at his feet. But such action was beyond him. He stayed where he was, shivering as if ill.

'Sweet Jesus,' he whispered, 'what is this? What is happening now?'

He shrank back into the shrubbery as McIsaac prepared to manhandle his barrow across the gurgling ground for another load. Cruachan watched him go, then went back to the factor's door. Blair opened it.

'Ye're late, Campbell,' he said abruptly. His eyes were evasive and his voice rough. 'I knew ye were too damned auld for the job.'

Cruachan hardly heard the words. 'What is happening, Mr. Blair?' he asked. 'The dear Lord knows you and me made a bargain yesterday for that path and now there is another man working on it over there behind them bushes.'

'Well, man, it's as simple as this—business is business,' Blair said. He saw with relief that there was more fear than anger in Cruachan's voice. 'That McIsaac came up here after ye'd gone yesterday and said he'd heard tell there was some work I needed. When I told him I'd gie'd it to you he said he'd do it for less. McIsaac's willing to make that path for fourteen shillings a day—and he's a gey sight younger man nor you, wi' mair work in him, or I'm mistaken. I'd have been daft not to tell him to start.'

'Fourteen shillings a day?' Cruachan gasped. 'Breaking up the big rocks and wheeling the bits to where the path is to be is hard, heavy work, Mr. Blair. Fourteen shillings is not a wage for a man doing that kind of work at all. There is not much a man can buy with that kind of money, anyway.'

Blair glowered. 'Ye can buy the same wi' it as McIsaac. And that's the position. There's enough work for two men there and if ye like to wheel round another barrow ye can start in right away and we'll forget ye're near a half hour late. But fourteen shillings a day is the rate. If a man's ready to work for that, then, that's what the job's worth.'

For a moment Cruachan stood in silence, his instinct urging him to decline the work. He hated the complacent assumption of victory that he could see on the factor's face.

Deep in his shabby body, under the neglect and indifference, something defiant still lived. But despite all his failings he knew that he must submit. There was Flora, the girls, the big brick house.

'Just show me the barrow, then, Mr. Blair,' he said. 'It is time I was started.'

5

CRUACHAN returned to the tin house that night numb with misery. His arms and back ached from the brutal effort of smashing the rocks and pushing his barrow over the sodden ground. But killing as this work was, he would have done it twice over if he could have been rid of McIsaac.

When Blair had shown him where to find the rocks for breaking and then left him, with barrow and sledgehammer, McIsaac had turned on him with a leer.

'Oh, it is yourself, Cruachan,' he said. 'Imagine you being working here as well. Man, man, is it not funny that the two of us should be working here together on the same job, and the pair of us cousins, as well?'

All day, as their barrows passed, McIsaac kept on. Cruachan had no defence. The man was impregnable. Argument he would have welcomed. Curtness bounced back uselessly. When at last the time came to finish, Cruachan had bounded away, exhausted though he was.

Behind him, as he squelched along with grim energy, he could hear the wheedling voice crying for him to slow down, beseeching him to display some comradeship and finally—when he continued to ignore it and draw even farther ahead—pursuing him faintly with furious curses.

The first thing he saw as he came into the kitchen of the tin house was the old deal table draped with a cloth and laid with unusual lavishness. The bread was sliced and stacked on a plate in the centre of the table instead of lying uncut on the bare wood as on a normal day. There was a spoon in the sugar-bowl. The milk was in a jug instead of in the can which usually stood on the floor at the side of the table.

Cruachan was so astonished by all this gentility that he did not make the customary uncouth rush that was his normal reaction to the sight of food after a long day in the open. As he tried to rid himself of the confusion raised by this domestic sensation he saw a man crouching on his heels in the shadows by the fire.

'O miserable and entirely unworthy Cruachan,' the figure intoned, 'even the heat of these peats is diminished by the chill of your despicable and maleficent presence.'

The voice seemed to give Cruachan sudden energy. He clapped his hands together and ran forward. He sank down on his knees on the dusty floor and peered into the man's face to convince himself it was really who he thought it was.

'Glory be!' he cried, clapping his hands again. 'Hallelujah! It is yourself, Abrach, sure enough. This is certainly the place in all the world where you is needed most. The dear Lord certainly knows where to send His messengers, all right. I am in need of the biggest comforting of the Lord that I has ever needed in all my life, Abrach, and the dear Lord knows that's true.'

Abrach made no recognition of Cruachan's delighted welcome. He stared sternly into the peats and started to sway on his heels.

'It sounds to me as if the dear Lord has been needed badly around this tin house for a long time, Cruachan Campbell,' he said, in a voice of mournful chastisement. 'The things I've been hearing about you Campbells is enough to make a man's hair stand on end. I've been hearing that you've been that lazy again that if ye hadna got this job at Finnoch Castle ye would all have starved to death. And ye've been refusing to sign the petition that Sandy McCaskill's got up, although every other man on Torrismore has put his name to it.'

His head shook despairingly and his voice was laden. 'I'm tellin' ye, Cruachan Campbell, the Lord will like neither of them things. They're both sinful. A man has a sacred duty to work for his family and no man has a right to stand in the way of his fellows, and that's what you're doing by refusing to put your name on that petition.'

He sprang to his feet and pointed a fierce finger at Cruachan. His voice rose. 'Of course, what you've done is just nothing to the terrible trespasses of Our Sheena, if only half the dreadful things I've been hearing about her is true, and her a missionary in the same holy order as myself.'

Cruachan seemed not to have heard. 'You will say a nice prayer for me, Abrach, sure you will?'

Abrach's eyes were fierce. He was typical of the dwindling band of sombre religious men who travelled the islands preaching a direful gospel to the scattering of stolid men and women who could still accept it. Twice a year he visited Torrismore, basing himself at the tin house because of its nearness to the mission hall and also because Cruachan never asked him to pay for the poor board and hard lodging provided.

It was over a week since Our Sheena's homecoming. The chill had quickly passed from her mighty body, driven out by the zestful forces that lived there. Now she came into the kitchen and, seeing Abrach standing by the fire, walked over to him and took one of his hands between her own. It might have been a gesture of simple friendship, for the expression on the girl's face was of warm, almost demure, tranquillity. But Abrach, as if her touch recalled some distasteful previous experience, recoiled.

'I wish ye would make this girl of yours stop touching me like that,' he said plaintively to Cruachan. 'I've told the lass a hundred times it's not any way for a lady missionary to go on, even she doesna mean anything by it.'

'The trouble is that Our Sheena has not been going on the way a lady missionary should at all or she would not be the bally way she is now,' Cruachan said. And then: 'You would not be knowing anything about how it happened yourself, now, Abrach, would you?'

Our Sheena laughed as if Cruachan were talking about someone else, but the missionary blushed and turned away. In the things of the Lord, Abrach felt sure and strong, but the grosser ways that Our Sheena knew so well turned him weak and afraid.

When the missionary had arrived some hours earlier Flora had bundled Grampa into the back room where he slept. Now, while all attention was on Abrach, the old man quietly opened his door, tiptoed across the room and lifted a slice of bread from the table. In recent years it was only by stealing that he had managed to live at all. Unfortunately, Flora chose this moment to come into the room carrying a boiled egg in a wooden egg-cup and she struck out at Grampa as he scurried across the floor clutching the bread to his chest.

'It's easy enough to see where this son o' yours gets his wicked ways from!' she shouted.

'It looks gey like it to me that you Campbells are just a natural sinful crowd,' Abrach said peevishly. 'I thought I could smell the awful stench of sin in the wind as I came round the bay this morning. If ye ask me, I'm exposing myself to some gey fearful influences by sheltering under the roof o' this auld tin house. I don't know why I do it.'

'Weel, I know all right,' Flora snapped, as she placed the egg on the table. 'I know without needing any telling. Ye sleep here because ye get your bed and your bite for nothing. But if ye think you're not safe in the tin house then ye know what ye can do.'

'Now, now, woman, don't you be going annoying Abrach before he has prayed a wee bit for me,' Cruachan said, trying to be angry in Flora's direction and placatory in Abrach's at the same time.

'After the things that have happened to me this day I'm in need of some Heavenly comforting. I want to hear from Abrach that the dear Lord knows I'm still here. I want to know, or I'll not sleep this night, that He has not shut the glorious and everlasting gates against me, like it sometimes seems He has.'

Abrach was plucking nervously at his eyebrows. He knew that outside the wind was blowing cold and heavy and that the next house where he might find shelter was a long way over the island.

'Och, there's no need for ye to get so angry with me, Flora,' he said, in the tone that he employed when he was about to take a collection. 'Ye maun know that the Lord and me likes all you Campbells an awful lot. I was only kidding on about being afeared of sleeping here. Michty, have I not been coming here these last twenty years, woman? Surely ye widna put me out after me being coming here all that time, especially when I was just about to get down and say a wee prayer or two for ye all.'

'Hallelujah!' Cruachan shouted, clapping his hands together and jumping up and down. 'I knew you wouldn't refuse me, Abrach. You know how heavy a poor man's sins hang on him, so you do.'

Abrach, who had not eaten since breakfast-time, was anxious to get at the boiled egg, and before Cruachan could say another word he flopped down on his knees.

'I can feel the holy praying creeping over me,' he said in a canonical tone. 'All them that wants to receive the comfort and absolution of the Lord shouldna delay a minute longer in getting down on their knees.'

When Cruachan, Flora and Our Sheena had settled on the floor beside him, with their eyes tightly closed, Abrach snatched a piece of cheese from the table and pushed it into his mouth. Then he began to hum softly. His congregation waited patiently, for they knew this was Abrach's way of attracting God's attention before he started.

'Please God,' Abrach said at last, 'this unprepossessing and entirely unsavoury individual would like to address You. I'm kneeling in the tin house at the Bay of the Angels in Torrismore wi' contrition in my heart for the trespasses and omissions of all Thy servants who are gathered here beside me. Ye'll no doubt recognize them. That's Cruachan on my left, Our Sheena on the right and Flora in the middle. Cruachan, it appears—and no' to my surprise, I may tell Ye —has been lazy as usual and neglecting his temporal as well as his spiritual duties, and now, of course, he's gey anxious for You to make everything all right so that if he dies through the night he'll get into Heaven all right. Ye maun know that Cruachan's a right sinful cratur, but he's confessed to me of his sins and promises to behave himself better in the future. Cruachan's on the side of the holy all right, though most times he gives cause for us ecclesiastics to doubt it.'

Abrach paused for breath, for inspiration and to swallow the cheese.

'Abrach certainly talks to God nice, doesn't he, Flora?' Cruachan whispered. 'You can tell he's well got there, all right.'

'Haud your wheesht, Cruachan Campbell,' Abrach snapped, 'I'm still in communication with the Lord.' Then bowing, as if to a vision, he continued. 'While I'm at it I would also ask Ye to deal leniently with Cruachan's daughter, Our Sheena, who, although she is one of Your missionaries, has been conducting herself in a gey irregular and disturbing manner.'

Abrach paused for a moment. 'The only thing I can say about Flora here is that she's a fine hard-working woman, as Ye must know Yerself. A fine body, indeed.' He started to rise from his knees. 'Amen,' he said.

He was already halfway to the table when Cruachan caught him by the leg. 'You hasn't said goodbye to the Lord like you usually does, Abrach. You hasn't ended up nice at all.'

Abrach made a squeaking noise and dropped down again like a sack that has been suddenly drained of its contents. 'That's all the praying I have to do just now, God, so bless us all and make us nice and holy for ever and ever, amen.'

He was on his feet again before Crauchan could delay him further, and in a single movement had seated himself at the table in front of the boiled egg. He clasped his hands and was booming out the grace before his kneeling flock had opened their eyes.

'O Lord, for this sumptuous feast, for this veritable banquet, I thank Ye, but only, O Lord, if the hen creature that laid this seed, this egg of life, was one of Your pure creations. If its life was in any way tainted by the filth of Satan and his malevolent forces, then I implore Ye, Lord, snatch away this shelled thing, cast it to the ground, use it, O Lord, as a thunderbolt to strike down and blow asunder Thine enemies.'

By the time they had finished eating and cleared the table the fire had burned low and the summer dusk lay over the island, spreading the rocky slopes of the mountain with mystery.

Cruachan began to get ready for bed. He struggled out of his rubber boots. He unbuttoned his trousers and hitched the braces off his drooping shoulders. When the hairy garments fell listlessly to the floor he stepped out of them, leaving them where they lay. Then he jumped quickly into bed still wearing his socks and shirt. He squealed as he pulled the cold sheets over him.

The big iron bed that he shared with Flora stood near the open stone hearth of the fire, not only for warmth but because Cruachan liked to be in a position to spit into the peats without lifting his head from the bumpy straw mattress. All their life together Flora had tried to stop him spitting from the bed.

'It's just no' right,' she had told him a thousand times. 'Nobody'll ever tell me a man was meant to lie stretched out in bed and spit into the fire.'

What worried Flora most about Cruachan's spitting was the fact that her side of the bed lay between him and the hearth. Flora never felt safe, for even when Cruachan was almost asleep he sometimes

44

decided he needed an emergency spit, and on these drowsy occasions his aim was never to be trusted.

When Abrach stayed at the tin house he slept on the floor in Grampa's room on a horse-hair mattress, although he had hinted at various times that he would have preferred the bed occupied by Flora and Cruachan.

'Hard lying is no strain on missionaries, cushioned as they are in the wondrous arms of the Lord,' Cruachan always told him.

When Cruachan stopped squealing at the coldness of the sheets Flora took off her sack and got into the bed beside him.

After a few minutes she lit her clay pipe and with an expression of great innocence allowed the smoke to drift over to the other side of the bed. Cruachan, who had been lying with his eyes shut, sat up with a shout and tried to strike the pipe from her mouth. When this failed he put his hands round her neck and shook her till her face was almost purple. Throughout this onslaught Flora kept her gums stubbornly clenched.

'By Hell, Flora, get that pipe out when you're in bed!' Cruachan spluttered. 'I'm not going to have you lying here puffing away like Christmas.'

Flora rubbed her neck and allowed another cloud of fragrant smoke to drift over him. 'Get to sleep or it'll be time for ye to get up,' she said, hoarse from the mauling she had received, but succinct as ever.

The cause of Cruachan's fury was not that Flora was smoking in bed, but that she was smoking at all. Two days before she had taken his tattered leather pouch, containing the last of the tobacco, and hidden it where he could not find it. Cruachan had been restless ever since, for until he could get started again on the big brick house, or until Roddy came home and helped him start a lazybed, his clay pipe was about the only comfort he had. Since Flora had seized his tobacco he had watched her with the gaze of a predatory animal. He had even followed her about the house in the hope of finding her hiding place. Once or twice he had struck her over the head and kicked her on the legs, but forty years as his wife had dulled Flora to such approaches. Cruachan still had no idea where the tobacco was.

'When ye come in here wi' your first week's money we'll see about the tobacco,' Flora had said.

Cruachan glared at her across the bed. 'When Roddy comes back with some of that good-smelling tobacco I instructed him to fetch, I'll make bally sure not a cut of it goes in that pipe of yours,' he said.

He punched the mattress a few times and put his head down; then he spat despondently past Flora into the peats.

In the back room Grampa was lying awake, planning to start early next morning on his coffin. When he was getting into bed he had noticed in the flickering candlelight that a disfiguring layer of dust had settled on it as a result of the religious activity that had taken place on the floor of the next room. Every so often the old man got up and lifted the coffin lid to satisfy himself that the bread he had stolen earlier was still inside.

In the kitchen Abrach had resumed his crouching position by the fire. Our Sheena sat on the floor gazing at him. The missionary kept his head averted, but he could not still the murmuring of his heart. Our Sheena put her hand on his knee. The paraffin lamp was turned so low to save the oil that she knew neither her mother nor father could see her.

'Is that yourself?' she whispered.

Abrach shivered, but he said nothing and made no attempt to move her hand.

'I would certainly like to go praying with you tomorrow, Abrach,' Our Sheena said. 'Would you like that, too?'

Her voice was soft and in the darkness it seemed to Abrach that she was suggesting something less laudable than prayer. The message that he saw glistening in the green of her eyes and felt throbbing

46

warmly from her hand was not of the spirit. His mouth was suddenly so dry, his senses so invaded by dark impulses, that he was almost speechless.

'The Lord doesna like men and women missionaries travelling thegether,' he said thickly.

'The Lord would surely not frown on me just for walking over the island with you a bit and carrying your bible like you used to let me do when I was a little girl just about a quarter or so as high as I am now, Abrach?'

Abrach's voice quavered. 'Ye're not a little girl any more, Our Sheena, and even worse, for the safety of your soul, ye're not even acting like a little girl. If ye go on saving men the way I hear ye have been then ye're going to ruin yerself in the eyes o' the Lord and be no more use to Him in His holy work.'

Our Sheena laughed in the shadowy light.

'You don't think I've been doing any wrong thing now, Abrach? Lady missionaries just naturally go about the saving of souls for the Lord a bit different from men missionaries.'

'Aye, its gey different from the way men missionaries go about things, all right,' said Abrach. He was staring fearfully into the mantle of white dust that now obscured even the warm remains of the peat. 'But it's not any different from sinning.'

The way Our Sheena was now stroking his leg appalled Abrach, but he could not make himself do anything to stop her. He was held like a fly in the bitter honey of sin. Our Sheena's voice slid ruinously on, uttering words so terrifying that Abrach wanted to scream a protest, begging Heaven to bear witness to the purity of his life and to absolve him of all blame in the crime that the girl's tongue was committing.

'I tell you it is not sinning, Abrach,' she said tenderly. 'Sometimes that is just the only way a man can be brought to the arms of the Lord. Sure as bees make honey, Abrach, and before the Lord, I tell you a man somewhiles needs more than spiritual comforting.

Spiritual comforting and prayers all on their lone are just not a bit of good to some men. Some men are so steeped in badness they just pays no heed to only kneeling praying. Kneeling praying just is not powerful enough to avert them from their sins and their wickedness and turn them towards the holy kingdom of the dear Lord. Oftentimes men needs that other kind of comforting as well, and that is what the dear Lord created lady missionaries for.'

Abrach could make no reply. In the darkness Our Sheena could not see the tears that fell from his demented eyes.

She spoke on with huge meaning:

'Sometimes a man needs that other kind of comfort without even knowing it, Abrach. That is why the Lord made me as big as a fir tree, so that when it is needed I can take a man right up and give him some of that other kind of comforting—even despite himself.' Her grip on his leg tightened. 'You understand that, Abrach sure you do, now?'

A queer forsaken terror possessed him. It was as if he were the last Christian on earth and the lions were closing in. Then, somewhere in the desolation, something stirred. Awkwardly, as if he were paralysed, his lips started to move. He had summoned a prayer, and now, with trembling sincerity, he pleaded with God to dispel the temptation, either by striking the life from Our Sheena or giving him the strength to hurl her away.

In the bed Flora had fallen asleep with the pipe still held tightly in her mouth. Cruachan was trying to get it without wakening her, but so far he had failed.

Our Sheena ignored Abrach's symptoms of distress.

'Why do you think the dear Lord made me this size like a fir tree, Abrach, if it was not to save for Him the souls of men who is too sinful to hear the holy words?' She moved nearer.

Cruachan, with a quiet gasp of triumph, managed at last to extract the coveted pipe from between Flora's obstinate gums. Joyfully he spat into the peats, so engrossed with the gratification of his own needs as to be heedless of the two figures only a yard or two from his side.

As if Cruachan's victorious spit had been the signal, strength burst into Abrach like a crusader. He jumped frantically to his feet, casting the girl's hand from his leg.

'I can tell ye, right enough, Our Sheena, why the Lord made ye as big as a fir tree,' he sobbed. 'It was to stop ye damaging yerself too much. As far as I can see, ye're nothing but a great big lump of sinful woman, and the Creator in His wisdom made ye the frightening size ye are so that depraved men wouldna be so ready to avail themselves of the terrible wickedness ye're carrying around with ye.'

Cruachan, drugged with pleasure, spat complacently from the mattress without moving his head.

'I has never seen a girl as bally big as Our Sheena, any direction I looked,' he said, chattily. 'No man I ever saw between here and the Coolins is going to think on marrying Our Sheena unless he has got a step-ladder, and the dear Lord knows that. I consider that is why He made Our Sheena a saver of men and a fisher of souls. By Hell, Abrach, there is hardly a man left on these islands that Our Sheena has not saved for the Lord, some time or other. When it comes to saving men's souls for the Lord that girl o' mine will work all day—or even all night—if it is called for. I've seen Our Sheena leave the tin house when the sun was still above the hill and it was full three o'clock of the morning when she got back. All tired and tousled up she was, but content, too, and with a kind of look in her eyes that would have made you a Christian just to see it.'

As Cruachan spoke, Our Sheena rose lightly from the floor and disappeared into the darkness.

Cruachan puffed clouds of ecstatic smoke towards the rusty roof.

For some minutes Abrach sat by the hearth, marvelling at the speed with which he had been released from the tyranny of Our Sheena's ardour once he had passed the dilemma to God. Then he went into the back room. He undressed quietly, without even lighting the candle, so that he would not waken Grampa. On the occasions when the old man was awake he kept Abrach listening for hours to the long recital of his miseries. Abrach considered that in the last hour he had known affliction enough to last him the whole night through.

Gratefully he lowered his weary but still inviolate body to the hard mattress. But a second later he sprang shrieking to his feet again.

'Sweet Jesus, save me!' he wailed, as he bolted through the door to Cruachan's room. 'Our Sheena's through there on that mattress!' he cried. 'The girlie maun be out her mind.' He shook Cruachan by the shoulders until the pipe fell from his mouth. 'Man, Cruachan, ye've got to stop Our Sheena. Nothing me or the dear Lord can do is stopping her. Ye've got to make her stop.'

Cruachan felt about on the bedclothes for the clay pipe so that Flora, who had been wakened by the noise, would not find it first. He felt that so long as he held her pipe as hostage there was a chance of his recovering the remains of the tobacco.

'Do ye hear me, Cruachan Campbell?'

Before Cruachan could answer, Our Sheena came into the room carrying her clothes. She went over to the door of her own room.

'Sure Abrach has no sense of humour at all, Daddy, to go shouting like that,' she said, toying with the long fair strands of her hair. 'I wish it had been light in that back room so I would have seen Abrach's face when he found me on that mattress.' She laughed and pointed. 'Abrach certainly looks funny standing there in his shirt-tail. Not many people would give a penny for Abrach's praying if they could see him standing there with the tail of his shirt all shaking in the draught.'

Abrach, who had been standing grey-faced and affronted at the side of Cruachan's bed, blushed purple. As he stood, undecided how to deal with this ribald and unrepentant defiance, Flora, her face

50

inscrutable, leaned out of bed and slowly lifted up the fluttering end of his shirt.

'I've aye wondered,' she said, her face solemn and speaking as if to herself. 'Aye wondered.'

With a gasp of terror Abrach fled blindly back to the sanctuary of his room.

When stillness returned to the house Cruachan, Flora and Our Sheena fell asleep immediately, but several hours passed before the missionary's eyes closed and peace came to him on the hard mattress.

6

CRUACHAN looked at his boat. The brittle carcass lay tilted on the pebbles above the tide-mark of black seaweed. He had abandoned it many years before when the steamer service had been withdrawn from Torrismore and his career as ferryman abruptly ended. The storms of winter and early spring had been seizing it ever since and smashing it down on the beach. Now it was stripped of every scrap of paint.

It had been Cruachan's intention for some years to give a little time to the boat, but apart from occasionally sitting on the pebbles and resting his back on the wasted timbers, or lazily twirling the rusty propeller screw with his foot, he had not yet made any move in that direction. Now, despite its deep state of decay, Cruachan had conceived a new and exciting future for it. When he grew his potatoes with Roddy he would sail them to Oban himself instead of paying the ruinous freight charges.

As he stood planning the details of this crafty move he heard the sound of weeping. It was a thin, convulsive sobbing that undulated across the desolate landscape in irregular waves, as if, having floated with some strength over the hill-tops, it then became lost in the glens.

Cruachan stood quite still and listened to the broken sound.

Suddenly a figure stumbled over the crest of a small hill. It swayed for a moment at the top and then started to run towards him with a distracted shriek.

It was Mairi Fiona.

Her hair, which she spent so many hours every day brushing into sleek patterns, was in wild disorder. She fell at her father's feet and lay there with her head pressed into the ground.

'By Goddy, Mairi Fiona,' Cruachan whimpered, 'what is this that has happened to you now? Tell me, girl, what has happened? Who is chasing you like this to make you run till you fall right down the hill?'

The child was shuddering hysterically and she answered Cruachan's call with a moan. He lifted her with careful tenderness and supported her against his chest. Her face was white and her brow was cut.

'It is your daddy, Mairi Fiona,' Cruachan said. 'It is your daddy here beside you and no one else. You are all right and fine now, but for the dear Lord's sake tell me what has been done to you.'

Mairi Fiona opened her eyes with fearful reluctance. 'It was Murdo Mhor!' she cried, rubbing at her tears and smearing her face with blood and the dirt from her hands.

'Murdo Mhor was it, then? And what did the foul devil that he is do to you? Tell me, now, girl, what did he do?'

Cruachan was shaking her slightly as if in sudden irritation, his alarm and solicitude diminishing, it seemed, now that she had actually spoken. It was as if, already, her distress offended him by its strident intrusion into the peace of his day.

Mairi Fiona looked up at him, searching for comfort. 'He touched me,' she sobbed. 'He touched me. Oh, Daddy, it was terrible!'

The child's body shook with another burst of weeping. She strained round in Cruachan's arms and looked fearfully up the hill as if her attacker might be lurking there.

Cruachan urged her remorselessly on.

'Oh, Murdo Mhor, was it? And what did that man do to send you crying like this? Tell me, what did Murdo Mhor do?'

'I was just passing his house from Kitty Campbell's, where Mammy sent me with a message, when he came to the door and gave me some chocolate to eat. Then he said he had a ribbon for my nice black hair and if I would go in he would give it to me.'

Cruachan's fingers gathered round her arm. 'You did not go into that man's house?' His voice was incredulous. 'I has told you a thousand times, and Our Sheena when she was young, never to go into the house of Murdo Mhor.'

'It was only to get the nice ribbon that he had for my hair,' Mairi Fiona wailed. 'He said if I came into the house he would give me the ribbon and then inside it was dark and he . . . he touched me. Oh, Daddy, I don't want to go near that house again!'

Cruachan did not take her to the tin house, but he stood watching until she had gone inside. For a few minutes more he did not move, but gazed over the croft to the lowering splendour of The Angels and the decrepit silhouette of the brick house. Then he turned and began to walk quickly across the island.

Murdo Mhor had the grey look of a man almost at the end of his time. He was the island's money-lender, the distiller of its illicit whisky and the most lecherous man in the place. Every year more and more crofters were having to ask Murdo Mhor to lend them money. It was the only way they could argument their National Assistance. Occasionally, when a man could not keep up the repayments, certain discreet negotiations were commenced. The result in a number of cases was that a new girl strongly resembling a daughter of the defaulting islander would be seen keeping house for Murdo Mhor.

Cruachan was one of the few men on Torrismore who was not in debt to Murdo Mhor. Often, when food had been so scarce at the tin house that it seemed they must starve, he had been tempted to walk across the island to the big grey house with the blank gables and small, secretive windows and ask for money. Flora, on occasions, had even pleaded with him to go, but a streak of perversity had held Cruachan back even in the days of his deepest misery.

Now he approached the house free of the stranglehold that its occupant had on almost everyone else in Torrismore. The door was opened by Murdo Mhor himself.

'Oh, it is yourself, Cruachan.' The crafty face was assembled into a fawning smile. 'It is a long time, indeed, since we have had the honour of seeing you on this side of the island.'

It was as if he could imagine no keener pleasure, but there was a wary reserve in his shadowy eyes as he pulled the door open to its widest extent. 'Just come away through and we will have a seat at the fire.'

Cruachan, who had experienced confusion at the first sight of the man, banished his uncertainty sufficiently to spit on the unscrubbed doorstep. It was a crude but expressive show of the feelings he had carried inside him since leaving Mairi Fiona.

'That for you, Murdo Mhor, and your fire and house and rotten white face,' he said like an excited child. 'Man, man, you should tie a knot in yourself instead of lusting about after young girls like Mairi Fiona. The dear Lord would prefer that, and, by Goddy, so would I!'

Murdo Mhor received this expression of loathing with an impassive bearing. He had a long time ago come to accept such demonstrations as part of the wages of his lechery. All he feared was a complaint that might bring the police over from Oban. He was impervious to all else.

'You can maybe do what you like with the daughters of some folk on this island but not with Mairi Fiona!' Cruachan shouted. 'I does not owe you a thing, so don't you go rolling after Mairi Fiona.

Don't you go touching that girl of mine again or I just don't know what I'll do to you.'

'I just don't know what you're shouting at, Cruachan Campbell,' the money-lender said. His eyes were wide with innocence. 'I just don't know at all. That girl of yours was here, all right, a while ago, but I just wanted to give her a ribbon for her nice black hair. That was all I wanted. I don't see any harm in that, just wanting to give her a ribbon.'

Cruachan spat again, pulling up the juice from the depths of his disgust and throwing it, this time on to Murdo Mhor's boots, with a sound as if he were vomiting.

'That is not what my Mairi Fiona told me,' he said in a quivering voice, 'and I am warning you now, don't go touching that girl again. I will get my children all the ribbon they need, even if I is poor, without you at all.'

'I was just going to tie the ribbon on Mairi Fiona's hair, that was all, Cruachan, when suddenly she ran away,' Murdo Mhor said in an outraged voice. 'And don't you go spitting any more. That's no way for a man to go on.'

Suddenly, as he stood watching the wheedling face, Cruachan began to wonder why he was there. All at once, as if the events of the last hour had been obscured by a drifting mist, the sullying of his child seemed insignificant beside the sharp memory of his own gigantic problems. They moved about in his mind like spectres, but so compelling that it seemed they must have been rooted in him at the moment of his conception. The brilliant optimism that had filled him as he stood by his boat only an hour before was now sterile and inert. A stupendous melancholy was creeping through him like a cold shadow. He longed with an almost unbearable intensity to have Roddy back so that they could start work together on the lazybed for next spring. Tears came softly into his eyes and trickled slowly down his face.

Murdo Mhor watched understanding nothing.

56

'Come into the house and have a dram like a friendly man,' he said uncertainly. Then, sensing that the tirade was over: 'You and me should be friendly, Cruachan. I've got a great big feeling that I could help you on a bit, if you would only let me, like the other folk do. It certainly sounds to me, from what I hear, that you and Flora could do with some help over there at the tin house.'

Cruachan stared at him sightlessly.

'Anytime you needs anything over there at the tin house, Cruachan, just you come and see me about it. There is not a man on Torrismore now who does not need a bit of help some time or another, and that's what I'm here for.'

All at once, in Cruachan's continuing silence, Murdo Mhor saw a force more menacing than the previous abuse. This sinister stillness seemed to foretell trouble of the kind he dreaded. His fear that Cruachan might send for the police returned. He knew that if this happened there would be no dearth of witnesses to speak eloquent evidence of his ill-repute.

There were many people—shackled by his vicious extortions— who would weep sweet tears to see him go—even if only for a few months. A bleak vision of how those months might be spent reared before Murdo Mhor's worried eyes. Somewhere in his brain a cell door clanged.

'Christ, Cruachan,' he blurted, servile and cringing with panic, 'I swear I never touched Mairi Fiona! All I was doing was tying a nice ribbon on her long black hair. You're the man I like best on all of Torrismore. You Campbells are the nicest people on this island and I just would not want to offend you any way. Young girls like Mairi Fiona get some queer ideas in their heads, even when there is nothing at all happening. But just to make everything all right and fine, Cruachan, I'll row you round a big cask of good whisky. I remember right well how you used to like a good dram and how you used to walk over here and buy a jug when things was not so hard. I'll row that whisky round and you and me will have a dram together for old times.'

Cruachan turned away. He had not even heard the man's last words.

7

FLORA waited until she heard the outside door banging shut behind Cruachan, leaving her alone in the house with Our Sheena. 'I'm asking ye for the last time,' she said, 'who's the father of this bairn? I'm your mother and I have the right to know, so I have.'

She stood limply in front of the girl, her arms hanging slackly at her sides, the lines of her peasant face quite expressionless. She spoke like a child who is repeating words that it does not understand and she looked as if she did not expect any heed to be taken of what she was saying.

Flora had so often in the last weeks demanded to know the father of her daughter's child that all force had long since left her voice. But, despite Our Sheena's evasions and secret silences, Flora could not stop trying. Sometimes she stood by Our Sheena's bedside as the girl slept, in the hope that a name might come from her lips during some dream of fond remembrance. On other occasions she would slink to within an inch or two of her daughter's back and then speak the question into her ear as if hoping by sudden attack to force an unguarded answer.

Our Sheena had many reasons for not speaking the name that her mother was so anxious to know. The chief of these was that she did not know herself. This fact had not particularly troubled her, but under Flora's interrogation it became almost the only thought she had; day after day she sat by the fire mentally shying away from the enthusiastic activity that it suggested. Remorse and self-pity flooded in; especially self-pity. No one wanted her. She was spurned by Abrach. She was giggled at by Mairi Fiona. She was ignored by her father. She was assailed by her mother. Most of all, she was afflicted by her conscience. Every day she became a little more withdrawn from this hard reality. *God is our refuge and our strength. What a friend we have in Jesus. Oh, what needless pain we bear.* Slowly she retreated into a dream world of biblical comfort and miracle. And gradually the *not knowing* was transformed into a tremendous possibility. The great theme that had implanted itself in Our Sheena's fevered senses played on hypnotically until at last it became a radiant conviction—and she was happy again.

'I'm asking ye for the last time,' Flora repeated. She seemed mesmerized by her own incantation.

Our Sheena remained silently aloof. She was deep in a wonderful speculation that had removed her in everything but physical presence from the tin house, the island and the very times in which she lived.

Flora looked encouragingly about the empty room. 'Come on now, Our Sheena, there's not a soul here but us two. Tell your mother what she wants to know. Not another soul will ever ken, cross my heart.' She licked one of her fingers and made a sign with it on top of a safety-pin that held her upper garment shut. 'Tell me before Dr. Munro gets here. This is the morning he sent word he'd be.'

Our Sheena did not speak. Imminent motherhood had put a warm bloom on the normally majestic gauntness of her face and there was at this moment a complacent simper of satisfaction on her rose-bright lips.

Flora could not bear her daughter's expression. She did not think it in keeping with her predicament.

'All right, ye big bitch,' she snarled, darting forward and shaking the ecstatic figure by the shoulders. 'Have your wee bundle without a name to it, and see if your mammy cares.'

As Our Sheena bent down with careful dignity to pick up the bible that the assault had knocked from her hand, Flora cackled like an hysterical witch. 'Hee, hee, hee, ye'll look a real picture of holiness going about preaching salvation wi' a wee bastard under your shawl, so ye will!' she cried.

Our Sheena was about to speak, but Flora was not to be interrupted.

'Tee-ee-ee, hee-ee. And who'll feed it, forbye?' she gasped. 'Your daddy can scarce fill our bellies as it is. Will your bonnie Assembly Wi' God and the Scripters and all that feed the wee bastard? Have ye thought of that?'

'The dear Lord has sent me this child and He will feed it,' Our Sheena replied, with the calm of a saint. 'He will look after us both. The Lord always provides for them that are on His right hand, especially the holy missionaries that devote their lives to the spreading of His glorious Word.'

Flora considered this pronouncement for a moment, and then, folding her bare arms across her concave chest, she made a sucking sound with her mouth. 'So it's the dear Lord, is it?' she sneered. 'Ye'll be telling me next it's the dear Lord that did it to ye.'

Our Sheena radiated sweet tolerance. 'There's no need to blaspheme, Mammy. The dear Lord has a terrible fate held in readiness for use in the after-lives of them that blaspheme.'

Flora had not lived so fully or experienced such intensity of emotion for years. 'Och, keep your sermons for some poor soul that needs them,' she jeered. 'You and that bone-lazy man that's your father rave on about God as if ye knew Him better than anybody else. God'll be the death of ye both.'

Our Sheena had retreated so far back into her sanctity that she did not hear anything of these last insults. She said, as if in continuation of what she had said some moments before: 'God sent an angel to visit me in a vision and then I was with child.' As she spoke, the girl joined her hands in front of her and there came into her face such a look of rapture that Flora backed away, baffled by this transfiguration and the extraordinary statement which had preceded it.

'Angel?' she said. 'What angel? What vision is this ye're raving about now?'

At that moment, before Flora could boggle further or Our Sheena elaborate, the outside door swung open. Dr. Munro swept heartily into the room.

'A grand day outside, ladies,' he smiled. 'A day to set the blood flowing and the heart singing, but come night it will be a time for the fireside and a book, I'm thinking.'

He sat eagerly down on the spindly hardness of the chair opposite Our Sheena. There was so much relish in everything the old man did that it was as if a sunbeam had suddenly shone out in a deep cave.

Our Sheena closed her bible and put it on the floor beside her.

'Oh, it is you, then, Doctor. Mammy and me were just having a wee talk here by the fire. She said you'd be coming this morning.'

'That's right, my big healthy-looking lass, but by the sight of your rosy cheeks and the sheen on your hair I needn't have bothered. The good nursing your mother gave you has had you up on your feet for many a day, I can see that.'

Flora, who in the time since Our Sheena's first painful night of illness had hardly spoken to the girl except in anger, accepted the compliment with downcast eyes. 'That's right, Doctor,' she said, smoothing her hands over the rough and gritty surface of her potato-sack skirt.

Dr. Munro seemed in no hurry to become professional. He looked about and listened to the rattling of the house like a man hearing again an old piece of music. 'And where's everybody this morning?' he asked.

Our Sheena resented his unaccountable failure to confine his interest to her own uniquely interesting condition. While her mother and the doctor talked she sat straight and still, sensing, with the yearning of a drunkard, the life inside her.

At last the doctor turned to her.

'Now, my lass, now that your mother and I have stopped wagging *our* tongues, I'll just have a look at yours.' He chuckled and squinted down at her. 'Fine,' he muttered. 'Put it back. Couldn't be better.'

Our Sheena suddenly felt less like a Madonna and more like the small girl who used to hang on the doctor's rucksack and swing along behind him as he walked round the bay.

'And how are you otherwise?' He smiled, trying not to embarrass her, but before Our Sheena could answer Flora spoke.

'I don't know what's come up wi' her at all,' she moaned. 'She just sits there, one day like another, staring at that bible and looking queerer and funnier every minute. She never moves, but just sits quiet and kind of smiling for hours, and never even turns a page. I wonder, whiles, if the girl's all there.'

The doctor smiled at her. 'It takes them all ways,' he said. 'All ways. You'll maybe remember that from your own time.' He got up, slapping his hands on his knees as he rose. 'Well, girlie, away and lie down in your bed till I have another look at you.

'Aye,' he said, when he had finished, 'it'll be a Christmas present to remember—or very near it, depending.'

A sweet radiance came on to Our Sheena's face; an emotion, it seemed, almost too fluttering and birdlike to have originated in a creature so large. She touched, almost gratefully, it seemed, the coarse sleeve of the old man's Harris-tweed jacket. 'That's right, Doctor, Christmas Day.'

The tenderness in her voice startled him. It was astonishing. They

63

were as promiscuous as poultry and yet when the harvest came they went as coy as nuns. He patted the hand on his sleeve.

'I didn't say Christmas Day, my dear, but more or less. I've been doing this now for fifty years and if there's one thing I've learned it's never to be dogmatic about the arrival of a baby.'

A queer smile came on to the girl's face. 'I know it will be Christmas Day.' Her voice was firm.

He laughed. 'Then what are you asking me for, if you know?'

'I just wanted to be sure, Doctor.'

He sighed. Consistency from the female, even under ideal lab conditions, was rare. He had learned that in his youth. What could one expect from one in the clutches of pregnancy?

He swung on his rucksack. 'Now there's nothing to worry about, lass,' he said. 'I'll be here with you in plenty of time, and if I'm needed before that you know how to get me.'

Our Sheena looked away. She did not speak.

As the old man stepped out on to the grass at the front door, Flora gripped him confidentially by the arm. 'I don't ken what's ailing the girl,' she whispered. 'Do ye know what Our Sheena says, Doctor? She says the father's an angel.'

Her eyes gleamed at the recollection of this alarming nonsense, but the doctor only laughed. 'I should imagine it's no uncommon thing for a woman to think that about the father of her child,' he said, 'although, of course, an old bachelor like me is no expert in that kind of thing.'

He laughed again. 'And you know, Mrs. Campbell, Our Sheena might be right. Anyway, she should know.'

'Na, na, Doctor,' Flora said, shaking his sleeve. 'A real angel, an angel from Heaven, like them out there, wi' wings and haloes and all.'

Dr. Munro blinked. 'I see,' he lied. 'That kind of angel. Most interesting indeed, Mrs. Campbell.'

He had never ceased to wonder at the weird spiritual and mental gymnastics that his fey patients were capable of. There never was, he reflected, any real possibility of a town man understanding the islanders completely. It was like trying to understand the dream world of a child. A man could only laugh, for, Heaven knows. for all you knew the devils might be having a sly laugh at you.

To Flora's intense disappointment the doctor did laugh. 'An angel, you say, Mrs. Campbell? I must write a short note to *The Lancet* about this. Yes, I should think they'd be quite interested.'

He patted her arm and became serious again. 'If I've any other calls over here on Torrismore I'll be looking in to see the girl,' he said. 'She's as strong as a horse, though. I don't think you'll be needing me before the end of the year.'

Flora retreated glumly into the house. 'The poor auld man's off his head,' she muttered. 'And so are you, my girl. All this talk about angels! I've just never heard anything like it.'

Our Sheena was not listening. Her smug and dreamy expression had returned. 'Did you hear what Dr. Munro said?' she asked. 'My son is to be born on Christmas Day.'

'Your son? So ye ken now it's to be a son, do ye? I suppose ye'll have a name all ready for it, too?'

'Yes, Mammy, I have.'

'Oh, have ye, now? Well, what is it? Or is your mother not good enough to know, seeing it's angels ye deal wi' now?'

Our Sheena looked down at the bible on her lap. 'Emmanuel,' she said. 'They shall call his name Emmanuel.'

The strangeness of the answer and the way Our Sheena said the words drove the anger from Flora and left her only bewildered.

'That's a name I've never heard before,' she said, shaking her head. 'It's not a name any of the menfolk on this island has.'

8

THE path at Finnoch Castle was laid in a month—half the time it would have taken if Cruachan and McIsaac had been working with gentlemanly island sloth instead of in a grim spirit of mutual hatred. Blair, the factor, was delighted. Not only had he cut the rate by more than twenty-five per cent, but the job had been finished fifty per cent quicker than he could have expected—or, more important, than his London-based employer could have expected.

At the end of each week Blair always made the same joke as he dropped the money into Cruachan's cracked and bleeding hands: 'Just remember the coolies in Hong Kong that I was tellin' ye about, Cruachan. There's far worse places nor Torrismore—but no' many.

Now unemployment was settled about Cruachan once more and with it had come the chronic indecision which had shaped his life. All morning he had been pondering his old problem—whether to get out his creel and look for some earth for his lazybed or go over to the big brick house and there work out some new plan for its completion.

He had walked studiously across the grass after breakfast like a professor of some old impoverished school and settled down with his back against the dry-stone wall and his face towards the warm, late September sun. He knew from experience that this was the position in which he thought most vigorously.

Across the sea the mountains of Argyllshire were wrapped in massive peace. In the softness of the morning the white peat reek rose only a foot or so from the chimney of the tin house and then fell to the ground, misting the croft with its sweet and flowery tang. Cruachan's head sank slowly downwards until anyone watching would have said he was asleep.

Flora was certain he was sleeping, for although she shouted to him several times to bring some peat and draw a bucket of water, he did not answer. But if Cruachan had known that his deep, reflective reverie was being mistaken for somnolence he would have denied it furiously.

When he wakened a dinghy was moving across the bay towards the pebble beach in front of the tin house. It was only when the small boat had grounded that he recognized the figure inside. It was Murdo Mhor.

Less than a week had passed since Mairi Fiona's terrifying interlude in the money-lender's parlour. 'What do you want here, Murdo Mhor?' Cruachan shouted.

The man smiled in his furtive way. 'Now, now, Cruachan, man, don't be sounding so unfriendly, and me just rowed you round here the thing I promised you that other day.'

Cruachan could not remember being promised anything, but for all his antagonism he could not ignore the astonishing words. He had brought him something. No one had given Cruachan anything but abuse and back-breaking work for as long as he could remember. Warily he walked down the beach, the pebbles crunching loudly under his boots. He was like a lean and much-abused stray cat advancing towards a saucer of milk held out by an old enemy.

The money-lender was pulling at a tarpaulin that covered something lying in the stern of the boat. As Cruachan arrived at his side, stiff with suspicion and embarrassment, he whipped the tarpaulin into the air like a conjurer reaching the climax of the vanishing-rabbit trick. There was a barrel in the boat and from it there came the unmistakable smell of whisky.

'There now, Cruachan, and what do you think of that grand sight?' Murdo Mhor asked. 'I told you I would row you round some whisky and, as everybody on these islands knows, I is not a man who breaks his word.'

Since the furious scene on his doorstep the money-lender had hardly left his still, so anxious was he to produce the potent bribe that he saw as the halter on Cruachan's tongue. The barrel of whisky was Murdo Mhor's offering at the altar of freedom. His fear now was that Cruachan, in the grip of some warped pride, might refuse it—as he had steadfastly refused the other allurements with which Murdo Mhor had enslaved so many others.

Cruachan's first crude instinct was to spit on the barrel, then on the face that was watching him with leery solicitude. But as he sniffed at the heavy vapours that came from the cask there rose within him a host of faint memories—like the tremors of an old love aroused again in a man by a breath of well-remembered perfume. In the distant days of his comparative affluence Cruachan, like every other man on the island, had regularly sampled the fiery delights of Murdo Mhor's *White Hearse*.

The money-lender sighed. 'I just don't know when it was now that you last came round and bought a jug of the old *White Hearse*,' he said. 'Nowadays not a man at all on the whole of Torrismore seems to have any money to buy a jug of my old *White Hearse*. No more! No more! That old copper still o' mine is green with neglect these days. That whisky there in that barrel would do the whole o' Torrismore a year and more these days. There is not many a man these days can wrap his tongue around a good big dram and feel it go down inside him, slow and yet terrible fast, warm and kind of holy, like nothing else a man ever knows in this life again after the times he leaves his mother's breast.'

As he sang this hymn to his own rough and corrosive waters,

Murdo Mhor lifted an oar from the boat and struck the cask a succession of shivering blows until the bung jumped out.

'Just smell that now,' he said, coaxing Cruachan towards the open bung-hole. 'Smooth as mother's milk and rich with the tang of malt and peat. Never a better dram than this have you tasted, Cruachan. I'm making it better now than ever I was before.'

Cruachan gazed down the bung-hole of the cask as if it were a window into Heaven. But as the fumes reached his nose he jumped back. As he gasped for breath, Murdo Mhor slapped him on the back.

'Oh, it is well seen how long since you have had a dram, it is!' he cried. 'You're just not used at all even to the lovely smell of it now. What you're needing right badly, Cruachan, is a wee sup o' the cratur itself to put you back in condition, for I remember you were one of the finest drammers in your day on the whole of Torrismore, and maybe all the other adjacent islands as well.'

Under this heavy wheedling Cruachan's resistance started to split. As if sensing the deterioration, the money-lender leaned into the boat and lifted a rusty baling tin from under the seat. Then, handling the heavy cask with expert skill, he manœuvred it round until a sudden gush of whisky surged from the open bung.

'Here now, Cruachan,' he said reverently, 'get some of this inside you and it is twice or three times the man you will be feeling afterwards.'

Cruachan, knowing even as he did it that he was betraying himself, took the disreputable tin and put it to his mouth with trembling hands. The undiluted spirit went over his throat and into his stomach with the same stunning comfort as of old—burning but bearable, anaesthetizing the centres of protest, soothing away everything except the seductive heat in a sudden explosion of the intestines. When the initial shuddering had passed he stood quite motionless, smiling at his recent enemy with a look of bewildered fulfilment, but not speaking.

It was Murdo Mhor who spoke. 'There is no man in the whole world that does not feel the better for standing on the outside of a good dram,' he said, manœuvring the cask and pouring one for himself.

Cruachan sighed. 'A grand drop of the cratur, right enough, even if it was you that made it,' he said, a faint simper on his lips, but his voice stiff. He was alert enough still to see and shy away from the sudden forgiveness that he was beginning to feel.

After a minute or two he took the tin that Murdo Mhor held out and drank again. Then he lifted a pebble and threw it out to sea with all the strength of his thin body. The plop it made gave him a vague, unaccountable satisfaction.

Between them they manhandled the cask from the boat on to the beach.

'There you are, Cruachan,' the money-lender said grandly. 'Every drop in that big barrel is yours. Now you and me can forget that wee misunderstanding that came between us the other day. It does not do for two gentlemen like us to be fighting each other. No! No!'

As he spoke he leaned his arms out behind him until they rested on the bulwarks of the boat, almost as if he felt suddenly unsteady.

A small pulse of avarice was beating now in Cruachan. He looked up at the tin house like a miser who fears that his gold may be in danger. 'By Hell,' he said anxiously, 'if Flora or Abrach sees this whisky they will pour it straight into the bally sea! Flora and Abrach don't like whisky at all. Now that it seems the dear Lord has unloosed some of His glorious treasure on me at last I certainly does not want Flora or Abrach getting their hold on it. The first thing I wants to do is get this good old whisky hided down somewhere right safe and sound.'

With grotesque deliberation he walked over to the barrel, tackling the familiar beach as if it were an ice-cap. As he went he sang in a low voice:

'*Since the Lord loves me I'm as happy as can be. My cup's full and running over.*

'And since the Lord loves me the best place for this nice big barrel of whisky is in the house of the Lord,' he said, giving it a loving slap.

The money-lender looked doubtful. 'Which house is that, then, Cruachan?'

'The mission hall. That is the house of the Lord around here until I can get the big brick house finished.'

The mission hall was a small stone building situated a few hundred yards along the bay. Between them they rolled the cask there. The heavy, studded door was never locked and Cruachan kicked it open with a disrespectful boot.

'Help me roll this bally cask down there under that old pulpit,' he gasped. 'That old pulpit down there is the finest hidey-hole I know. Abrach will be climbing up into it to give us a right good sermon before he goes away from Torrismore, but nobody ever goes inside—except me.' He giggled at this revelation and then bent unsteadily to the cask again.

The inside of the mission hall was even more forbidding than the outside. The high, cold walls were of undressed stone and in places they were green with damp and moss. A few rows of rickety wooden benches stood unevenly on the stone floor facing the pulpit. It was like the inside of a crypt.

Since the island had no resident missionary, the hall was unused except on a few Sundays a year when Abrach preached his farewell sermons. Behind the pulpit, hidden from the congregation, was a door which led into the space under the steps. Cruachan opened the door and put his head inside.

'By Hell,' he said, 'this bally pulpit certainly is the finest little place the Lord ever made! Some days when Flora is all angry I get in here and stay here until she gets in a good state of mind. Flora just never thinks of looking for me here.'

They pushed the barrel inside and then stood supporting each other.

'Cruachan, you and me is the two finest gentlemen on this island,' Murdo Mhor said. 'The two finest. That little bit of trouble we had is all over now. All over. It's the little bits of trouble in life that brings people together.'

9

IT WAS the last day of September. After months broken by rain the sun shone over Torrismore, warming the white pebble beach, crackling through the gorse, sustaining the human hope that might otherwise have perished in the sorrow of another barren harvest. It was a morning when, elsewhere, men with good earth were opening it and lifting out the things they had grown.

Cruachan had never seen good earth, because on the island there was none. Nevertheless, he knew that somewhere in the world good earth must exist. He could not imagine a world in which good earth did not exist somewhere. To him, good earth was of the same sacred structure as air and light, and although he had never encountered any, he thought he knew how it would feel. Cruachan felt that a handful of good earth would be like the touch of God. Once, when he was sitting against the dry-stone wall, it had occurred to him to ponder whether he loved the earth more than he loved God. For a time this strange speculation had troubled him, but in the end he had decided that there was no difference at all between God and the ground and that he loved them both equally.

Cruachan's own peat earth was so irretrievably waterlogged and lifeless that even his neighbours shook their heads sadly when they walked by. When he opened it black water trickled out. When he planted things in it the roots rotted and the plants died. Every time he tried the same thing happened. When the time for the harvest

73

came the plants had gone. Only Cruachan's love of the land remained.

He had been certain that this year he would have had a lazybed on which he could have grown some potatoes. On a lazybed of dry and airy soil the roots would not rot. The plants would live and grow. But again, because of the inescapable pattern of his life, he had been delayed.

Now, as he sat with his back against the wall and the warm beams of sunshine touched him, he was filled with an insistent desire to break open the ground. He sat quietly for a few more minutes. This had been his cautious, life-long practice. He did not believe it wise for a man to act in haste. But, strangely, there came to him this morning none of the usual reasons for further delay. Everywhere he looked the sky was blue. There was no rain, and no sign of rain, in any direction that he turned.

He got to his feet and walked across the grass to where his creel lay. He picked it up. For the first time in memory there was no hole in it, nor any other reason that he could see for not using it. He walked round to the back of the tin house. His spade, warped and tarnished with inactivity, lay propped against the rusty wall, exactly where it should be.

He could not understand this smooth progress towards destiny. It seemed that nothing could stop him now. He walked, almost on tip-toe, across the croft till he came to the spot that he had selected for the historic enterprise. It seemed that the whole island was hushed as it waited for him to start. With a last nervous glance upwards, Cruachan positioned his spade on the black earth and raised a reverent boot. Before he could bring it down there was a wild cry behind him.

'O despicable Cruachan. O miserable Sabbath-breaker. Put down that accursed spade before the Almighty strikes at ye with shafts of lightning and tongues of diabolic fire.'

It was Abrach. He bounded balefully to Cruachan's side and tore

74

the spade from his hand. 'Pitiful son of Satan,' he shouted, 'is there no depth of iniquity or appalling unseemliness to which ye will not burrow? Six days the dear Lord has provided ye with for labouring, and on the seventh He asks that ye keep it holy. O Cruachan, I was sure ye loved God more than this, that ye would lift a filthy spade and dig at the ground on the Sabbath.'

Cruachan lifted both his hands and slapped his forehead. 'By Hell, Abrach, I forgot!' he exclaimed. 'I forgot this was the Sabbath morning. I was just sitting against the wall there thinking how good it would be to work the earth and the next thing I knew I was stooping over it with that bally spade.'

Abrach's face was grim. 'The Lord an' me 'll not stand for a man working on the Sabbath,' he said. His voice was sombre.

Cruachan dropped to the ground and rubbed at the grass with servile fingers. 'I never digged the ground at all, Abrach, just look,' he said. 'I was just about ready to open it a bit with the spade when I heard you yelping. I certainly am glad you got me in time.'

'Good men always remember the Sabbath,' Abrach said. 'The Sabbath is the only day of the week worth a man remembering. When a man starts forgetting the holy Sabbath I consider it's high time he was dead and done wi'.'

Cruachan was still holding the blades of grass hopefully apart so that the missionary could see the inviolate earth. 'I never digged it, Abrach,' he whimpered. 'I just never digged it. The dear Lord knows that.'

'It looks like this slimy island's needing a right good preaching to,' Abrach said. 'The sooner it's twelve o'clock noon and the utterly loathsome people that live here on this malodorous Torrismore get themsel's collected over there in the mission hall the better for their immortal souls. Yince a man starts forgetting the holy Sabbath the dear Lord's likely to rear up in His glorious righteousness and start unloosing His fearsome darts in all directions.'

The sun was even warmer now. More than ever Cruachan longed to lift up his spade and open the earth, even though he had no plants to put in it. Even though he knew that if he did have plants to put in they would die. In a moment of startling perception he knew, not only in his head, but in his heart, that Abrach's message was untrue.

'Why does the dear Lord not want me to dig the earth on a Sunday?' he asked with sudden truculence.

'Because Sunday's the Lord's special day, Cruachan. You know I've always preached that.'

'But why does the Lord let a man open the earth on a Saturday and get angry if he does it on a Sunday?' Cruachan asked with mutinous persistence.

'Because Almighty God created the whole great world and everything in it in six days, like the Good Book says, and on the seventh day, which was the Sabbath, He rested because He was tired from His great labours. That's why good people don't work on the Sabbath, Cruachan, so they can be like the dear Lord who didna work then neither.'

'It just does not make any sense at all to me, that doesn't,' Cruachan said. 'If the rich and the poor alike has to not work on the Sabbath, and if even the dear Lord Himself put down His tools and rested on that day, then why has all the missionaries and preachers taken the Sabbath for the doing of their work?'

Abrach's manner was as hard as the pebbles on the beach. 'Us missionaries are not going to lower ourselves to answer the likes of these wicked questions from the putrid lips of abominable Sabbath-breakers,' he said. He took a menacing step forward. 'We're here to tell the sinful and the unholy what they have io do to save their miserable black souls from the everlasting smoke and flames that the devil is mixing up doon below.'

Cruachan, although he sensed his peril, could not desist or retract. 'It seems to me missionaries like you and Our Sheena just go

76

about telling people what not to do. If you ask me, what missionaries should be doing is telling people to love God, and not just God, either, but the flowers and birds and rabbits as well, and not just that either, but the holy earth they walk on and every other bally thing in this old island. That's what I think.'

Cruachan had never spoken to a missionary with such audacity and he was frightened when he saw the terrible anger that he had raised in Abrach. The missionary's face had turned the colour of bell heather and when he spoke the words came from him like the sound of a high sea hurling itself into a cave:

'If ye pursue this course o' evil that ye're riding so hard,' he snarled, 'I'll have no option but to ask the Lord to throw all them sins right back on you that I interceded wi' Him to remove from your worthless soul the other week.'

This was the worst threat he could have made and the brutal quality of his voice gave it a terrible power. In an instant Cruachan's rebellion was over. Fear rushed in. He dropped to his knees again.

'Look, Abrach,' he implored, 'I never digged it at all. The earth's whole, but if I had digged it you are right. It would have been the worst sin a man could ever do and the dear Lord and you would have been right in punishing me as hard as hard could be. All you good missionaries do the right thing, all right, keeping us sinful people from spoiling the glorious Sabbath for the dear Lord by going around digging up the earth with spades.'

Abrach stood very straight and still, marvelling at the power his Lord had given him to strike fear into transgressors. For a moment or two he allowed himself to savour Cruachan's misery. He was pleased at having encountered and so triumphantly routed the devil at such an early hour in the morning. It augured well for the farewell sermon that he would preach in the mission hall later in the day.

Some minutes were passed in silence while the acid was allowed

77

to sink through to Cruachan's marrow. Then the two men walked back to the tin house, one filled with a glow of pride, the other no longer enjoying the sunshine.

Cruachan was still feeling crushed when he arrived at the mission hall with Flora at noon. But as he stepped inside all further thought of his argument with Abrach left him. The building reeked of whisky. For days the decrepit cask under the pulpit had been slowly leaking until now the air of the small hall was charged to explosion point. Around the hall the islanders sat in stunned and befuddled wonder, bemused and confused by every breath they drew.

Two men, more daring, more curious than the rest, had quickly traced the source of the delectable aroma. In almost frantic disbelief at their good fortune they had struck the bung from the cask and gulped deeply of the raw and undiluted spirits. Now, their eyes glistening, they emerged, still half wondering if they were experiencing some ecstatic hallucination. They sauntered casually to their pews, trying to appear as if they had been engaged on some legitimate official mission, striving to keep from their faces the small smiles of doped fulfilment that threatened to betray them.

Guilt and panic churned in Cruachan's stomach as he moved into his seat. He could sense the stiff astonishment in Flora as they sat down. The atmosphere of the hall, as well as being laden with whisky fumes, was now vibrant with expectancy as the congregation waited for Abrach to enter.

At last he came, the door bolted behind him, his boots striking dismal sounds from the stone flags. The congregation kept their eyes to the floor, but they could sense the growing dread in Abrach's progress. It seemed that his feet were moving with reluctance.

'It fills me wi' sorrow to say it to ye, brothers and sisters, but I've never smelt such a sinful gathering in all my years wi' the Assembly.'

When he reached the pulpit steps he shuddered as if something unclean had touched him. He turned a tortured face to the people. His voice was grave but strong, and his expression that of a man who knows that peril lies ahead and yet goes forward to meet it with fortitude. 'The devil's so strong in here that he's gripping my throat and nipping my nose wi' his unwholesome and accursed hands even before I can climb up there into my pulpit to do battle wi' him for the Lord.' As he spoke, Abrach put a foot on the first step of the pulpit and stood like a knight about to mount his charger.

'If ye ask me it's going to take some praying and preaching before it's safe for the dear Lord to descend on us in all His unbelievable glory here in this mission hall today. Aye! Some preaching and praying, for, Lordie me, brethren, I've never been in the thick o' anything like this afore.'

The noon sunshine was beating through the windows directly above the pulpit. Every second the gathering heat was releasing denser concentrations of vaporized whisky. They enveloped Abrach like sin as he went grimly up the steps. When he reached the top his face was ghastly. All over the hall people were whispering and in the confusion another two men went under the pulpit.

Abrach emptied out the collection and then began to count, flicking the coins back into the box from the pulpit ledge. He always moved the coins slowly because he could not count quickly, but today he seemed to be counting more slowly than usual and several times the coins missed the box and landed at his feet.

'This box'll just no' keep steady at all today,' he muttered, blinking as if a cloud were forming not in his eyes but behind them. 'Auld Nick's settled in here so well that mine eyes can scarce see through the hellish mist o' his appalling effluvium.'

Now that the door was firmly closed the volatile spirits had filled the air to saturation point and beyond. So far beyond that in some dark corners the etherized whisky was condensing back to a fine dew on the cold stonework.

'Four shillin's and sixpence ha'penny,' Abrach's voice said mournfully. Always before he started to preach it was his habit to announce the amount of the collection. Invariably when he mentioned the small sum donated he managed to convey hurt nobly borne and then it was his custom to stare down sadly at the guilty faces. On these occasions Abrach always saw himself on the cross. But today, despite the melancholy of his voice, there was a smirk on his face. As he looked out at his shuffling flock there was a sudden commotion in the shadows behind him. The two men who had been applying themselves to the bung-hole of the whisky cask had at last desisted—only, it seemed from their expressions, because they could not take another drop. As they walked to their seats one of them fell over an outstretched pair of feet and tumbled to the floor. He lay grinning for a few moments before rising.

In various parts of the hall men eased their collars and women moved nervously in their seats. They knew that something extraordinary was happening but they did not know what it was. Abrach emptied the contents of the collection box into his hands and then awkwardly stuffed the coins into a pocket of his jacket. He looked puzzled.

'I just don't know what's happening,' he said, 'but right here in my own pulpit, rising right up from these sacred auld boards, I can smell the terrible stench o' the Pit. The Pit is the awful place where the devil lives, brothers and sisters, and I can tell ye it's no' nice at all down there wi' all the bodies burning and the souls of the damned shrieking and yelling out for mercy and a drink of cold water to cool their roasting bodies. But a man shouldna be able to smell the Pit in his own pulpit like this. It's just no' Christian or holy any way I think on it. Yince a man can smell the Pit there's just no reason I know to stop Auld Nick himself coming a-galloping and a-walloping in the door.'

Steadily, the fumes kept on coming through the floor of the pulpit and entering the missionary's already half-paralysed brain.

Abrach had never felt such a weight of wickedness pressing on him before and there was a great desire in him to hurl his bible up the aisle and run for the door.

His voice rose suddenly and echoed round the hard walls. 'If ever folk needed saving it's you crowd down there,' he gasped. 'The devil's got such a grip on the necks of ye all that the whole of this poor mission hall's bunged up wi' the foul reek of brimstone. Lordie, lordie, me, I've never had to thole anything like this before!'

Abrach paused and screwed up his face as the unseen peril wrapped itself ever more terrifyingly about him.

'Let's kill the auld devil, brothers and sisters!' he shouted desperately. 'Let's grind his leprous face in and gouge his staring red eyes out wi' a wee quick hymn.' He held his arms outstretched as if he were about to lead a great orchestra. 'All thegether, now. Raise your voices for the Lord. Kill that auld devil.'

> *'With Abrach to glory,*
> *And nothing to pay,*
> *Saints and angels*
> *Guide our way.*
> *O' we're coming over,*
> *Over to glory,*
> *With Abrach to glory,*
> *And nothing to pay.'*

One of the men who had been under the pulpit giggled to his neighbour, took out a comb and wrapping a piece of paper round it blew a reedy and unmelodious accompaniment.

All around the hall women were weeping or squirming in their seats. Fire and brimstone had been hurled at them all their lives but never with such force. A group of crofters who had seen the second contingent of men emerge so happily from under the pulpit had gone to investigate the cause of their mysterious but enviable pleasure. And like them they had thrown themselves whole-heartedly at the irresistible maw of the barrel, their arid systems craving the well-remembered solace of Murdo Mhor's *White Hearse*.

Now they came out simpering with stupefaction and wound an unsteady path back to their seats, crossing the floor with the ludicrous concentration of men totally befuddled.

Abrach looked at them with bleary surprise as they went past.

'Praise the Lord,' one of them called to him, his inbred capacity for slyness beating even the alcohol.

'Kill that old devil!' cried another with the same cupidity.

Abrach took fresh heart from this evidence of the way his preaching had aroused the people. He liked to hear them crying out and singing, and even, if possible, to see them rolling on the floor.

Cruachan was sitting with an expression of petrified fear on his face. He was terrified that somehow Abrach would be able later to trace the cause of this chaos to him. Several times Flora had nudged him and whispered in a scandalized voice: 'Michty me, whatever's happening? Are they all drunk, or what? And Abrach as well?' But Cruachan had remained silent and continued to stare stead-fastly downwards with closed eyes as if engrossed in a long prayer.

Abrach could not understand why so many men were leaving their places and walking round behind the pulpit, but whenever he twisted round to see where they were going he always found the hall behind him bafflingly empty.

> 'With Abrach to glory,
> And nothing to pay,
> Saints and angels
> Guide our way.'

Under the pulpit men pushed and jostled one another in their anxiety to get at the cask. Some of them lay on the sodden floor and tried to get their mouths under the jet from the bung-hole. Others with more scientific minds took their caps from their pockets and used them to catch the whisky. Men who did not have caps caught the whisky in their hands and splashed it into their mouths in quick, choking movements. The intelligentzia took off their boots, filled them and drank like gentlemen.

Those men who had been under the pulpit sang with new and thunderous fervour when they returned to their places and as the hymn ended one crofter threw his cap in the air and cried out:

'Altogether now, brethren, once again!

> 'With Abrach to glory,
> And nothing to pay.'

A long black straggle of hair was swinging across Abrach's forehead as he tottered about the pulpit, besotted by the infatuating fumes. He threw out his hands as if warding off something unwholesome and when he spoke his voice was weighted with doom.

'O the wickedness that must have stalked this isle o' Torrismore,' he intoned. 'O the deadly sins ye must have nurtured in your licentious bosoms. Only the darkest abominations of the night could have released the cruel, evil beasties that's enveloping us now. I've never smelt the auld devil so strong afore. Never! I can feel the damnable sting of his fiendish breath a-nipping at my nose like winter. Kill that auld devil, brothers and sisters! Get hold of him by the tail and bang his shocking brains oot against the floor. The dear Lord would like that. The Lord doesna mind a bit of bashing and bloodshed so long as it's the devil. Kill that auld devil in your hearts, brethren, because that's where the dark yin lives. Inside your hearts Abrach can see the smoke o' the Pit curling up like a thundercloud.' He threw out his hands dramatically to indicate all the hearts beating in the hall. 'In all these hearts Abrach can see the foul and fearsome flames o' Hell. These flames are a-burning and a-roasting for you. Aye! For you, Mairi Sarah MacDonald, and for you, Donald Calum MacKenzie. All these wee individual Hells are burning away there for the devil, and it's your terrible sinning that keeps them lit. Ye're all burning there in front o' Abrach's weeping eyes like paraffin lamps on the road to Hell. Every time you wicked men sneak oot there in the bracken wi' some lassie ye're not entitled to, the awful flames leap a bit higher and hotter and the auld devil rubs his scaly hands and gurgles doon in his ulcerous throat like a drain. It's the same wi' all you women there when ye go prettying yerselfs up to get the men a-pawing and a-scraping at the ground.'

A man came out from under the pulpit, which was visibly quivering under the effect of Abrach stamping on the boards and hammering the ledge with his hands. He dried his lips on the sleeve of his jacket and went up the aisle with his hands in his pockets, whistling casually to himself and trying to look as if he were not there. But Abrach saw him.

'I just don't know what's going on, but maybe there's something doon here behind this pulpit I should ken about,' he said. He came down the steps unsteadily, but before he could get behind the pulpit two crofters seized him by the arms and another kicked the cupboard door shut.

'Man, Abrach, we just cannot risk letting you go in there at all now,' said one. 'Hamish McIvor is in there wrestling with a terrible big beastie that the devil sent. We might lose Hamish, but we just does not want to lose you, Abrach. We wants you out there in front leading on the praying and singing against Auld Nick himself.'

Abrach, who regularly struggled with the devil on the floor of his room before getting into bed, nodded understandingly. 'Kill that auld beastie, Hamish!' he shouted like an officer. 'Praise the Lord.' Then he dashed back up the pulpit steps.

The man who was making music from his comb had climbed on to his seat. His feet were tapping like a fluter's and he was blowing at the comb as if he were at a ceilidh.

'Keep it going, brother,' Abrach called to him. 'We've got to bludgeon the auld devil and gouge his staring red eyes out and there's no better way to that than a wee hymn.'

Under the pulpit the cask of whisky at last ran dry. It was like the sun finally setting at the end of a perfect evening. The men who were there and saw the last sad trickle experienced a sense of irreparable loss. It was minutes later before they could force themselves to leave the scene of their bereavement and return grieving to their pews.

Around the man with the musical comb some others were beating time with their hands.

'Hand in hand with the Lord we go.'

By the time the song had been performed twice more Abrach's flailing arms had struck his bible from the pulpit to the floor. His water glass lay shattered beside it. His eyes were red and glazed and his black tie was dangling outside his jacket. Rheumily he surveyed the hall like a shell-shocked commander. The man with the comb had played himself into unconsciousness and he lay silent now like a heap of rags. The singing had become broken and irregular, like the sound of distant rioting, as the singers slumped into exhaustion. During the last bout of frenzied melody some of the women had taken fright and had crawled to the back of the hall and run home. Now the door lay open and from the sea and the hills clean air blew in like oxygen. Abrach gulped at it like an asthmatic.

'We've done it, brothers!' he cried. 'We've done it, sisters! We've bashed the auld devil that hard he's had to scoot back to the vile Pit from whence he came.'

'Praise the Lord!' someone shouted.

'Glory be.'

'The old devil is killed! Long live Abrach!'

Abrach held up his hand for silence and then struck the ledge of the pulpit a crashing blow.

85

'Lusters!' he shrieked. 'Liars! Fornicators! Unhallowed and un-sanctified wretches! Ye brought the devil to your hearts wi' sin and wi' your filthy wallowings ye kept him there. Abrach and the dear Lord have cleaned ye up. Now repent! Repent ye now, I say! Squirm. Grovel. Writhe. Cry out in horror and penitence.'

He lunged forward. For several seconds he hung perfectly balanced on the pulpit ledge, then slowly his head went down, his feet came up and he toppled limply into the void, his mission accomplished.

10

GRAMPA CAMPBELL was dismayed. As the autumn days sped on, spreading the island with brown and brittle decay, vitality was sparking through his shabby body. Everywhere he looked there were signs of finality and rest, of life surrendered or taken back. The year was dying, but he was still unwanted in Heaven, full though he was of years, poor health and earthly weariness.

About a week before, in the bracing sharpness of the October weather, Grampa had become aware of an increasing lightness in his step and an even keener bite to his indomitable appetite. He had spent several days brooding on the injustice of these ill-omens. Now, more resentful than ever of his intolerable longevity, he was defiantly busy again with his macabre pastime of preparing for death.

He had left the tin house early in the morning after eating a bowl of porridge that was as cold and soggy as the island itself. His intention had been to continue his search for a piece of ground which might be suitable for the site of his grave. The old man had a horror of being buried in the sea, as, in his young days, many of the island people had been; and he hoped to avoid this by preparing now a place where he could lie, dusty, perhaps, but dry.

'It just is not Christian for a man's body to be lying under the waves,' he kept telling Cruachan. 'A man was never meant to end up on the bed of the cold sea with the weed a-swaying and a-twisting round him like big worms. The trouble around this tin house, though, is that the earth's so wet a man just can't dig himself a good dry hole, any way.'

The land all around the tin house was scarred with long excavations where Grampa had tried at various times to dig a dry grave for himself. He had been engaged on this quest for almost as long as he had been working on his coffin and there were now scores of discarded graves about the croft, most of them filled with black peat water.

Despite the grim energy that Grampa had lavished on this task he had not yet found a grave that pleased him. Invariably, when he started digging on an area of ground that looked hopefully dry, he would come on solid rock two or three inches under the surface. Often, as soon as he sunk his spade into the earth, black, oily water oozed out around the incision. On other occasions the earth was deceptive and Grampa would labour on until before him there lay a trench long and deep enough for his coffin, and still dry. When this happened he would dance up and down with perverse glee and shout to Cruachan or anyone who could hear him. 'By God, it looks as if I've got a dry lie at last!' he would cry. 'I just knew the Lord would not let me go on digging for ever and strike nothing but that old black peat.'

Sometimes, before Grampa had even finished rejoicing, the water was beginning to ooze out of the surrounding earth into his trench, gurgling wickedly at how it had deceived him.

Occasionally it took days before the sly trickle started. Once, during a summer drought, a grave that Grampa dug remained dry for ten weeks of almost unbearable suspense. Every night the old man knelt at the edge and prayed to God to keep it dry. Ranged against him on that occasion were the pleas of the crofters, who during that summer found themselves confronted with the unprecedented necessity of praying for rain.

In the end, after withholding the rain long enough to burn the crofters' crops, the sky opened with a shriek of derisive laughter and filled Grampa's grave to overflowing.

Sometimes the food that he received from Cruachan was so poor that for long periods he did not have enough strength to dig. During these spells of lassitude, which raised in him the false hope that at last he was going to die, Grampa worked at his coffin. For the last year all that it had required was an occasional dusting, but the old man's morbid urge to attain the black pinnacle of perfection would not allow him to stop. Whenever possible he took it out of the tin house on to the grass to give it an airing, for he was terrified that woodworm would get into it or that it would be attacked by dry rot. He would stagger out of the door under the weight of the solid oak, lean the coffin against the wall and kneel down in front of it as if he were going to pray. Then he would get out his duster, spit delicately on the wood and rub at it in small circles till Cruachan threw a stone at him or threatened to chop the coffin down for kindlers.

At last even Grampa himself realized that the wood was as smooth as it could be made and he had thereafter sought new ways of adding to the splendour of his creation. 'I wants to arrive up there so grand that the Almighty just won't have the heart to turn me back, no matter how sinful I've been down here,' he said in his thin quaver.

He had taken four brass knobs from the bedstead which lay in the grass outside the tin house and screwed one at each corner of the coffin so that it now stood on four highly polished feet. He had next cut six lengths of rope from an old anchor line and teased them out to form tassels which he had fixed to the coffin with solemn pride.

For several hours this morning Grampa had slowly walked the familiar landscape with his spade. His efforts were as frustrated as ever, but the activity helped him digest Flora's deadly porridge. After a while he walked down to the shore and started to rake about in the pebbles for shell-fish that he might eat. Now, as he stood gazing down at the beach, he saw among the pebbles and rocks something faintly gleaming. It was a small metal plate with a hole in each corner. On one side Grampa could see some faint lettering. He rubbed the metal on his trousers and then tested it for flexibility between his fingers. He wondered if it were gold. He had once heard of a man on the other side of the island finding a golden object on the beach. If one man had found gold on the beach surely this might be more? He looked about to see if anyone had seen him, and then, having placed the plate carefully in his pocket, he hurried back to the tin house.

For more than an hour Grampa worked at his treasure with polishing cloth and soap and water, and at the end of that time the plaque shone out brightly, a warm, glittering thing in the darkness of his life.

Grampa's polishing had also revealed the secret of the writing. The inscription on the plaque read—*Gentlemen Lift the Seat*. Grampa could not read, but he knew that a man did not have to be able to read to appreciate such beauty. In the old man's eyes the brass plaque held an almost ecclesiastical dignity, and because he felt that even God would be impressed by so much glory he screwed it on to the lid of his coffin.

II

SINCE Our Sheena's statement about the angel Flora had been too baffled to approach the girl again and the intercourse between them was now confined on Flora's part mainly to taunts and disgusted mutterings and on Our Sheena's to a frosty aloofness.

As the days went by, Mairi Fiona watched her sister with increasing wonder. 'I don't like the look of Our Sheena like that at all, Mammy,' she said to Flora one day. 'Is she going to get any bigger? I hope I never have a baby if it's going to make me as fat as that.'

'Haud your wheesht, ye stupid wee bitch,' Flora shouted. Then she pushed Mairi Fiona into the back kitchen to help with the washing-up. 'If ye ever have a bairn like Our Sheena, without being married, ye needna bother ever coming back here, for my heart's just about roasted out me as it is, wi' the worry and shame of it all.'

Cruachan was even less purposeful, and on the days when he could not find an hour or two's work at the lodge house, or over on Linga, he spent his time staring across his empty land as if imagining it flowering with the rich vegetable growth that he was determined to raise there when Roddy returned to help him. He wished Roddy would hurry back with the things he had told him to buy. There would be a lot of good eating there, when it came.

Each member of the family dwelt in the small world that each had created as an alternative to the harshness of their reality. They revolved round the ramshackle sun of the tin house like cold spheres in a remote part of the universe, never meeting, never touching, for ever sailing past one another in blind unconcern.

November came.

Our Sheena hardly stirred from her chair at the side of the fire. The bible which lay always on her lap and the journeyings of her mind gave her all the diversion that she needed.

Flora continually wondered about her daughter's air of placid fulfilment. It was galling to her that she could never discern in Our Sheena anything akin to regret. If the girl's expression ever lapsed from sweet repose it was to one of delightful excitement. Flora saw herself as a devoted and sacrificing mother, and what she longed for, to bolster this spurious image, was a weeping and penitent Our Sheena who would confess the full origin of her sin and then beg for her mother's forgiveness. Flora knew every move of this tender drama, for the words were by her alone, she took both parts herself, and the whole charade was enacted in the private theatre of her mind to an enthralled capacity audience of one—also played by the nimble Mrs. Campbell.

She would have been shocked to know that Our Sheena never thought of her at all. The girl felt need for no one. She was sustained by dreams. For Our Sheena the tin house hardly now existed. As the other members of the household huddled round the glowing peats in the dark winter nights, she walked the dusty roads of another land where the air was gently warm.

Sometimes Our Sheena made her journeys through this ancient land on the back of a small, mournful donkey. Wherever she went the people stopped in their labours and stood bowed in homage, and when she had gone, having given them her tranquil smile, they returned to their work uplifted, the women to sing as they swept, the men to repair their nets with new heart.

But on a dry morning of sun and sharpness in the third week of December Our Sheena made a real journey. She rose abruptly from her chair at the fire, put on her coat, went out of the house and hurried along the track. Halfway round the bay she left the path and stumbled over the uneven ground until she joined another track that led to the house of Calum Campbell, a cousin of Cruachan, and one of the less impoverished islanders. She avoided the front of the two-storey house and disappeared among the out-buildings behind it. A few seconds later, having met no one, uttered no sound and made no attempt to enter the house, she returned to the path and walked home.

Her child would soon be born and she was ready now for the whole great scheme.

When she came into the house Cruachan was standing in the middle of the floor dressed in a navy-blue suit, a black tie and a blue shirt.

Flora picked a white thread from the sleeve of the jacket and then stepped back to see how he looked. 'Ye'll do,' she said without emotion. 'But can ye not straighten up a bit? Ye're getting awful humfy-backed.'

'It's a puzzle to me that I can stand up at all with the terrible afflictions the dear Lord has sent me,' Cruachan muttered.

'There's Our Sheena standing there, big as a horse, just about ready to disgrace us.' He almost believed, as he said it, that her pregnancy was a matter of deep scandal on the island.

'It is no disgrace what the dear Lord sends,' Our Sheena said softly. There was in her voice, as always, a suggestion of something which eluded him.

As he stood baffled by the odd simplicity of her answer, she smiled across the room at him as if in forgiveness.

He turned away and pulled his boots from under the bed. 'I'd better give these a good clean,' he said, 'so I can step in to see Sir Eric feeling nice and smart. I don't want him having any bally excuses for not seeing me, like dirty boots might be up at the big lodge.'

93

When Cruachan left the house he was swept along on the sharp beauty of the scene. A white winter light lay over the island. Around the black mountain-top some mist trailed elegantly. There was an energy in the air that made every breath like the taking of something holy. He felt that on such a day there was no end to what a man might do.

All Cruachan's hopes as he went round the bay this morning were centred on Sir Eric Prentice, who owned not only the land on which the tin house stood, but the entire island of Torrismore. Sir Eric, who was Conservative Member of Parliament for a constituency in the Midlands of England, made his money from brewing a beer that was sold in almost every pub in the British Isles. Twice a year he brought large parties of guests to the island to revel with him for a few weeks at the big red-stone lodge. It was to the feudal ritual attending Sir Eric's arrival that Cruachan was now going.

Although, like every other man on the island, he detested his rich landlord, he dared not be absent. Cruachan earned a few pounds a year odd-jobbing at the lodge house and he knew that he would lose it if Sir Eric's agent noted his absence from the sycophantic throng when the lord of the island stepped ashore.

He had never before worn his good clothes in Sir Eric's honour, but today it was his intention to see the great man personally and ask him, once again, for permission to collect the seaweed that the tide threw on to the island shores.

Sir Eric had bought the island five years before and he made an impressive show in public of fighting the crofters' cause. 'My wild Hebridean home,' he called the island, in his Yorkshire accent, during his Parliamentary oratory. His real wish, however, was that Sandy McCaskill would be successful in his campaign to have the island evacuated. On the excuse of carrying out non-existent experiments in bracken control, Sir Eric had proscribed great stretches of the island and had told the crofters that they must not gather earth there for their lazybeds or walk across it even for pleasure.

He had forbidden them to take seaweed from the shore to fertilize their land. All his life Cruachan had been going down over the slippery rocks with his creel strapped to his back to cut the seawrack with a sickle, and it filled him with bitter bewilderment to think that Sir Eric could make it a crime for him to take up the seaweed that he was sure God put there for him to use.

One day he had met Sir Eric on the track outside the tin house. He saluted in the deferential manner that the man liked and then stood with his cloth cap clasped in front of him.

'I just can't think why you don't let us poor crofters use that seaweed there, Sir Eric,' he said. 'This bally peat soil just has not the strength to grow a thing but old bog grass unless we dig a good dose of seaweed into it.'

Sir Eric had looked at him silently for a few moments and then said: 'What the Hell are you talking about, man?'

'You shouldna be stopping us from lifting up the seaweed the dear Lord sends to make the earth grow some potatoes,' Cruachan had said. 'There is some things a man has a right to, and seaweed is one of them.'

Sir Eric, whose displeasure could cause panic in the offices of his companies in fourteen different countries, frowned. But Cruachan, waving his cap about, swept heedlessly on.

'There's plenty of seaweed there for us all,' he cried, 'but what loss would it be to you, Sir Eric, if us poor crofters lifted every bally shred the waves bring in? You don't need it up there at the lodge. You don't need any bally seaweed.'

The hairy tufts on Sir Eric's cheek-bones twitched. 'That seaweed's mine,' he had said very quietly, 'and I don't need any advice about it from a loafer like you with the heather growing out his ears.'

'I consider that seaweed there belongs to the Lord and He sends it up here on the waves for us crofters,' Cruachan persisted. 'That seaweed's not yours at all, Sir Eric. It's ours.'

Sir Eric could stand no more. He whacked Cruachan across the shoulders with his stick. 'If I catch you or any more of these bloody crofters stealing my seaweed I'll have you in court for it!' he shouted. 'This is my island and I own every bloody rock, pebble, lump of peat and shred of seaweed on it.'

After this black interlude Cruachan had waited fearfully to hear from McKinnon, the agent, that he would no longer be needed for work at the lodge. To his astonishment, he was engaged as before when the need arose. He did not have the subtlety to realize that Sir Eric's great fear, when he regained his calm, was that he might be charged with assault.

Nine months had passed and now Cruachan was ready to make another plea for seaweed. He could not imagine Sir Eric still refusing. He had convinced himself that the wild scene of the previous spring had been caused by some foolish misunderstanding that could now be resolved with good-natured ease. He pictured himself standing by the fire in the laird's library stating his case, and the other bowing in gentlemanly submission, and then, perhaps, thrusting a dram on him before he left.

When he reached the jetty the *Sea Star*, Sir Eric's steam yacht, was just gliding across the bay to her anchorage, every inch of her new white and yellow paintwork gleaming sleekly and the brass glowing like gold. When the anchor chain had rattled out, a pinnace was lowered. Two seamen in uniforms cut by Sir Eric's own tailor stationed themselves in her with movements as drilled and formal as those of men in a battleship being reviewed by a monarch.

Next, the bare fat leg of Sir Eric himself was edged over the side, where it hung, while he recovered his breath, like a laboratory specimen of an Eastern disease. It was the signal for Neil Campbell to squeeze a scream of weird sound from his bagpipes. As the wild note groaned over the water, Sir Eric jumped with fright. His fat back end wobbled under his kilt. Only the delicately placed hands of a seaman stopped the pendulum movement before it sent him plunging downwards—an event which would certainly have sent the pinnace to the bottom of the bay.

When Sir Eric recovered enough balance to continue his descent, Neil skirled his pipes into the heroic but inapt air of 'Bonnie Laddie'. Then 'Glorious Chieftain', as the laird was transferred to the jetty with a seaman braced behind him and the agent pulling from the landward.

When his score or so guests were arrayed behind him, twittering at the quaintness of the scene, and the islanders distributed mutely in front, Sir Eric made his traditional speech.

He started as usual with 'My fellow islanders'. As his ardour increased the metaphors became more muddled, the similes more inappropriate. Many times he referred to the great efforts he was making to help them all. At last he reached the climax.

'I told Sir James,' he intoned, 'that if this fair island of Torrismore dies, then Britain herself will die. And, moreover'—he paused— 'and, moreover, I told him that any nation that allows this little rock of ours to perish would richly deserve the extinction that would assuredly follow.'

The lunatic words ended at last. The faint memory of them echoed back for a moment from the rocky hillside and then drifted away over the bay to merciful oblivion. A wonderful silence flowed over the beach like a wave of warm oil. For a few moments the relief was so intense that no man moved. Then, as the beauty of it penetrated Neil Campbell's ear-drums, he hurriedly swung his pipes into position and set off in stately style to lead the march to the lodge.

When the procession arrived at the lodge it was met by two servants, one holding a tray of glasses and the other equipped with a supply of whisky. The agent led the crofters in drinking a ceremonial toast to the laird. And then—begone! For after this alcoholic climax to the cavortings Sir Eric wanted no more of them until his departure.

Cruachan lingered behind as the islanders hurried down the drive. When the crunch of the red blaes under their rubber boots was only a distant murmur he turned and looked back at the big house. It was a daunting sight, with its dozens of deep-set windows, its mock battlements and the great flight of curving stairs sweeping up to the big door, on either side of which two stone griffins crouched.

The exquisite lightness of spirit that Cruachan had experienced as he walked round the bay was gone. What he felt now was apprehension.

Electric lights, powered from Sir Eric's private diesel generator, were being switched on all over the house as the cohorts of servants, who had arrived a week earlier, led the guests to their rooms.

At the same instant there came to Cruachan a picture of his land —sodden with moisture, littered with boulders, crippled with in- fertility. He felt towards it two bewilderingly opposed emotions— the fierce, protective instinct of a parent and the desperate longing of a lost child. Resolutely he marched up the drive, climbed the staircase of winding stone and pulled the black metal bell-handle. After a long interval a manservant in formal dress opened the door.

Cruachan hurriedly took off his cap, so awed was he by the splendid figure.

'I would like to see Sir Eric,' he mumbled.

'Yes, and what is your business?'

Cruachan scraped his feet about on the step. 'Business? I has no business,' he blurted. 'I'm Cruachan Campbell from the tin house round there, the other end of the bay.'

The butler's body went stiffer.

'What do you wish to see Sir Eric about?'

'I wants to see Sir Eric about getting some seaweed for my land.'

The man blinked. 'I'm afraid the master is not to be disturbed at present,' he said. 'He is resting after the journey and won't be down until later.'

Before Cruachan could say another word the door was firmly closed and he was left standing on the doorstep with the griffins. Slowly there flowed into him an angry resentment. He would not be chased away. He wanted to dig his ground and he wanted to lace some seaweed through the black peat as he went along. He knew he would not be happy until he could sit in the house and picture the rich weed rotting down into food for the starving earth.

In the evening he again went to the door. He could hear music being played inside and the sound of men and women laughing. His heart was thumping as he pulled the bell and waited.

Almost immediately the door was opened, this time by a girl wearing a black dress, a stiff white apron and a semicircle of starched white linen on her head. 'I'm Cruachan Campbell from the tin house and I'd like to see Sir Eric,' Cruachan told her. He was delighted not to see the butler.

The girl went away and when she came back after a minute or two there was a smirk on her pert face. She indicated to Cruachan that he should enter. Cruachan felt his limbs weakening. He was overwhelmed with uncertainty now that the moment he had planned and waited for all day was actually approaching.

The sound of music and singing was louder now. The words of the song came clearly to him.

'Why should I cry in the wilderness,
The wilderness of my aching heart?'

In a corner of the shadowy hall he saw a girl in a dress which reached downwards to the floor but in the upwards direction stopped midway between her waist and her shoulders. She was giggling to herself and tottering towards a long corridor, and on her head there was an orange-coloured paper hat.

The servant girl led Cruachan across the hall to a big double door of waxed oak. 'This way,' she said. There was an odd expression on her smooth young face. She pushed open one of the doors and stepped into the room. As Cruachan followed his ears were filled with a violent confusion of noise. Above it all came the relentless singing voice.

*'All joy gone. No light left.
Only an aching heart.'*

It was the most terrifying moment of Cruachan's life. He stood stricken into immobility, his head slightly forward, one arm half raised, his legs bent and quivering. The room was seething with men and women in evening dress. Most of them were laughing loudly. On their heads they had paper hats, and in their hands glasses from which the contents spilled and splashed on the floor as they jostled one another in their merriment.

The room alone, empty of people, would have been enough to overawe Cruachan. It was long and distinguished, with panelled walls, a carved fireplace, in which birch logs imported from the mainland burned fragrantly, and a high ceiling decorated with gold leaf. At one end a Christmas tree soared gracefully upwards from a tub, its dark-green leaves brilliant with fairy-lights and artificial snow. Holly hung on the walls and paper streamers of gay colours were looped about the room. One entire wall was lined with buffet-tables laden with cold meats, punch bowls, pickled fish, trifles and cheeses. Behind this massive display two men in blue and white checked jackets and tall white hats stood ready to carve, scoop and spear at the bidding of the guests. Servant girls hurried about the room with trays of drinks.

In any part of the room where they could find sufficient space couples danced to the smooth flow of music which came from a gramophone in a mahogany cabinet.

> *'Why should I cry for tenderness,*
> *Tenderness for my aching heart?'*

Cruachan gaped for a moment at the whirling figures in their fine clothes, and then he swung frantically round. He wanted to rush out through the door to the freedom of the night. But the maid had closed the door and behind him Sir Eric himself now stood, a glass of whisky swilling in one hand and a cigar in the other. He was winking at the nearest of his guests, who were staring in surprise at Cruachan's peasant figure.

'Well, Mr. Cruachan Campbell, and what can I do for you?'

Cruachan was so embarrassed that he could not answer.

Sir Eric puffed. 'Well, man, speak up. What d'ye want?' His eyes were sparkling. He knew the reason for Cruachan's visit, for the butler had told him of the earlier call, but he wanted to make him explain it so that they could all hear. He remembered Cruachan well from the springtime.

The crowd gathered round.

'Well, well, well?' Sir Eric's cigar was waving in front of Cruachan's white face. 'What d'ye want to see me about? These are my friends. You can speak freely in front of them, you know.' He guffawed and cigar ash fell down his jacket. He took another glass of whisky from a passing waitress.

> *'Hoping for peace.*
> *Waiting for love.*
> *The prayer of an aching heart.'*

The crooner rotated into silence, leaving the room peculiarly hushed for all the noise that was still going on in it.

Cruachan managed to speak.

'I came to see you about seaweed, Sir Eric, but you're too busy.

I don't want to talk to you about seaweed now. I just want out to go home to the tin house and Flora.'

Dizziness was in his head. He tried to push his way to the door but Sir Eric's hand stopped him.

'Seaweed?' he said. 'Seaweed? But this is Christmas, man. The season for holly and mistletoe. Not seaweed. Oh, no, not that.'

The guests nudged one another and sniggered into their drinks. They did not understand what it was all about, but there was something in Cruachan's face that stimulated them. It reminded them of the chase. It was almost like hunting. Only this time it was a man they had. They yelped about him like hounds. They had no pity. Pity? Hell, if he was anything like the fox, the fellow would enjoy it.

Their happy laughter and gay shouts dinned in Cruachan's ears.

'Seaweed, my dear. What on earth next?' said one scraggy woman to her partner.

'The man wants seaweed,' squealed another. 'Did you hear him? Has anyone in the house got a bit of seaweed?'

'Is this a wee Hielan' Santie Claus ye've goat furr us, Surr Erric?' cried a small man whose cummerbund had risen up round his chest.

Amid the joviality Sir Eric advanced on Cruachan.

'Have a cigar, Cruachan Campbell.'

There was hysterical applause as he jabbed his own cigar at Cruachan's mouth. The soggy end split open against Cruachan's teeth, filling his mouth with strands of tobacco which stuck in his throat and burned his tongue. He spat them out and looked about for some break through which he could run. But there was no way out. They were pressing in on him in a suffocating deluge of starched shirts, bare bosoms, jangling jewellery and French perfume.

Sir Eric's jacket was open now and his tie was squint. He emptied his glass. 'Have a gargle, then, if you don't appreciate good tobacco,' he bawled. 'Manson! Give this fine Highland gentleman a large whisky.'

The crystal glass that the butler thrust into Cruachan's hand fell through his fingers and shattered on the floor. As he stared stupidly down at it, someone pushed a paper hat on to his head.

'Let's all drink to *seaweed*,' Sir Eric bellowed, beating his hands on his belly as if it were a drum. 'Seaweed, seaweed, glorious, glorious seaweed,' he sang.

The shrieking throng took up the marvellous refrain, and then, joining hands, danced round Cruachan, who stood trembling, with his eyes closed.

'Seaweed, seaweed, glorious, glorious seaweed,' they roared, till the streamers swayed and the holly fell from the walls, dislodged by the thumping of their feet.

Someone seized Cruachan by the hand and swung him into the cavorting crowd. From one to another they whirled and pulled him, the jagged studs on his skidding boots tearing deep gashes in the beechwood floor. At one stage of the mad dance he realized that both his hands were free and with a burst of hope he started to run for the door. He had gone only a few yards when a pair of bare arms wound themselves round his neck.

'Don't go yet, you old darling,' a girl's voice said. 'You must dance with me. You must!'

It was the girl he had seen tottering in the hall when he came in. The orange-coloured hat was still perched crazily on her long fair hair. 'Dance, you old darling,' she giggled, trying to manœuvre him about the floor. The shoulder-straps of her low-fronted dress had slipped halfway down her arms. Now in her struggle to make Cruachan move the thin straps snapped and the dress fell to her waist.

The crowd cheered louder than ever, but Cruachan, in a new surge of panic, hurled the slight, drunken form away from him. She slithered across the floor, hit the wall and lay screaming. Instantly the crowd turned to her.

This time Cruachan reached the door. He opened it, clattered across the hall, opened the other door and hurled himself into the darkness. At the far end of the driveway he stopped running. For several seconds he stood bent double with his hands on his knees. Then he was sick.

When the sickness stopped he stood shivering for a while. Then he started the long walk home. Behind him the lights of the big house shone brightly and the sound of laughter and music followed him.

12

OUR SHEENA had stubbornly continued throughout her advancing pregnancy to wear the uniform of the Assembly with God as Father and the Holy Scriptures as Law. Despite the wild incongruity of this get-up, despite the ribald comments thrown at her by Flora, she solemnly dressed each day in the grey skirt and jacket.

The securing of the skirt had presented a problem of increasing difficulty, but at last the limits of elasticity and compression were reached. No amount of tugging, no application of pressure, would allow the skirt to be worn. As she stood with the garment in her hand, Our Sheena looked down, as if noticing her appearance for the first time. It was the only part of the miracle that caused some stirring of puzzlement to drift through her otherwise impregnable obsession.

It seemed wrong that so special a life as that which she carried within her should result in anything as grossly material as the disfigurement that now spoiled the lithe outline of her long body. She dallied with the paradox in a remote, almost bemused, way. Could it have been like this . . . then? That first time . . . in Bethlehem? Could a God emerge from this?

Her hand moved slowly over her body, almost as if seeking to erase what was there. She was astonished to hear herself saying in her head: *Oh, Lord, take this Chalice from me*. Then, slowly, the returning delusion obliterated these stirrings of reality. Again her hand moved over her body, but caressingly this time. 'Emmanuel,' she whispered. 'I love you, Emmanuel.'

When she came out of the room she was wearing an ordinary dress.

Flora watched her through rancorous eyes. 'It's about time that ye tried to hide yerself,' she said. 'Ye've been going about like a shameless big hussy long enough, disgracing your father and me. I've been frightened to meet anybody when I went out, for fear o' what they might say. It hasna been decent, the way ye've gone strutting about in that tight skirt as if ye were proud o' what ye've done.'

Flora looked obliquely across the room. Then she lowered her eyes and shook her head mournfully. 'It's fair terrible.' She sighed brokenly, as if the outposts of her endurance had been reached, and passed.

'But I am proud, Mother.' Our Sheena's voice was sweet. 'I'm as proud as proud of what the dear Lord has sent me.'

Flora scowled. 'The dear Lord had nothing to do with it. Do ye expect me to tell folk it was the dear Lord or an angel that did this to ye? All this religion and preaching has gone to your head, if ye ask me. If ye had spent as much time reading the Bible as ye do now, ye wouldna be in this pickle of bother. Ye wouldna have had the time.'

Cruachan moved in his seat by the fire. 'Shut your whining, woman,' he called across the room. 'I'm trying to rest me here for a minute before going round that big bay out there to see if Roddy's on the mail-boat, but there is no bally rest I can get with you and Our Sheena there.'

'The whole of Torrismore is talking about the disgrace o' it,' Flora went on. 'That auld bitch Kitty Cameron stopped me the other day. "Oh, good day now, Flora," says she, as nice as ye like, "and how are ye all keeping at the tin house? Give my congratulations to Our Sheena. I didna know she was expecting. I didna even know she had got married, but news travels awful slow on this island, does it not, Flora? Has her husband no' come home wi' her, though? I havena seen any man about?" '

Flora waved her hands about loosely, like a black and white minstrel. 'That's the kind of terrible things I've got to listen to because you've been going on like a big hoor.'

For a second it seemed that Our Sheena might thrust out her large hands and seize her mother's wrinkled neck, but instead the beatific smile struggled on to her face. Then she walked slowly away. She could, it seemed, endure anything, so deep was her sanctity. 'I will pray to the Lord to forgive you for the awful words you have just uttered, Mammy,' she said with terrible charity.

Cruachan rose noisily to his feet. 'Well, hoor or no hoor, it is time I was away or I will be late for this mail-boat I'm expecting Roddy on,' he said.

He blew through the cold and empty pipe which hung dejectedly from his gums. 'I certainly am going to enjoy a puff of that good-smelling tobacco I instructed Roddy to fetch,' he muttered.

Flora did not hear him. When he left the house she was still staring, like a vengeful scarecrow, at the door of the room into which Our Sheena had retreated.

Roddy was not on the mail-boat, but two strange men were. They were city men, harnessed in hard collars, stiffly mounted in formal clothes as if for a business conference. The other crofters who had come to meet the boat—shabbily dressed men with the same distant expression as Cruachan—managed to note every detail of the strangers' appearance without actually facing them.

Cruachan heard the two ask the way to Sandy McCaskill's.

The boatman, a broad, wind-battered mariner in seaboots and several layers of high-necked jerseys, tumbled a bulky packing-case from the boat to the jetty. He looked down complacently at the label which declared the contents to be fragile. 'If that boy of yours doesna hurry back soon, Cruachan, there is going to be nobody here,' he said. 'Them two there going to Sandy McCaskill is Government men from Edinburgh come to see about moving all you bally crofters off somewhere else.'

Something cold and rigid entered Cruachan's chest. 'Them Government men has been coming here to Torrismore for years and years and they just never does a bally thing, except talk and make bally promises.' His voice was strong. 'Anyhow, Kenny Macdonald, them people is not God. Them people cannot move a man off the land if he does not want to go. The dear Lord just would not let them do that. By Goddy, I never signed any bally petition for getting moved off this island. I'll be standing here when Roddy gets back, all right. Don't you wory about that, by Hell!'

Cruachan's voice had grown so loud that it could be heard all over the bay. His thin body shook. He whirled round on the jetty, away from the confused boatman, to face the collection of shabby figures on the darkening beach.

They watched him in wonder.

'By Goddy, you people don't know what ye're doing!' Cruachan shouted. 'You people there is just being led away by what Sandy McCaskill tells you, and not working things out in your own brains like the dear Lord would want you to. Every other while Sandy McCaskill comes around by the tin house asking to get me sign on a long sheet paper for getting taken off this island; but I is not for signing and never will. . . . No! Never will! I'm like that old heather there. Every year it comes a-shoving and a-pushing up through the peat, but you move that heather to some other ground with no peat and it will come up no more. People is the same. The dear Lord does not set a man down in peat if it's some other ground he needs.'

He was filled with an enormous desire to convince them of their folly in wishing to desert the land that had given them birth.

'By Goddy, why can't you men grow a few potatoes like me and Roddy's planning on raising once he gets back from the mainland

and we get started carrying some earth for a lazybed?' he shouted. 'That is what a man is meant to do out here.'

He scanned their embarrassed faces for some sign that they were getting his message.

A man in a patched navy-blue jacket, his pale face twisted and lined as if by years of anxiety, waved his hands at Cruachan in excited dissent. 'It is all right for old men like you, Cruachan, to talk, but the people who has left this island is doing themselves fine in the towns now. Their children has got jobs in shops and offices, 'stead of sitting around here, staring at the rocks and the bracken and waiting for something to grow up out the earth that never does come, ever.'

Another man stepped forward and glowered at Cruachan as if he had suddenly been revealed as the architect of their misfortune. 'That's right,' he shouted, 'the folk that has gone does not need to get up no more at five of the morning to milk an old dry cow or haul some seaweed up the beach quick before Sir Eric's man sees them or the next bally tide comes in and drags it all back again! The people that has left here has got houses now that don't go clang in the wind like that old tin house you Campbells live in, and they does not starve with their bellies empty in the winter because the boat canna reach them with food, either. I consider I agrees all the way that they should take us all off this island—and I'll tell them men in the black coats that if they ask me.'

A rumble of approval came from the other men and the clicking of the pebbles disturbed by their feet echoed strangely over the bay like heavy rain.

Cruachan was looking over their heads. If they could, his arms would have encircled the whole desolate vista—the bare rocks, the yellowing grass, even the great hard mountain itself—crushing them all to his breast as proof of his inexpressible love.

His voice was desperate. 'The Lord certainly has made things hard for us poor people out here on this island, but I consider He has stood me out for special attention. The Lord has set me down on the wettest bit of peat earth in the whole world, I think, and the biggest crop of rock man ever saw. Every year I gets poorer and poorer till sometimes I wonder what the dear Lord is playing at. I go twisting my brain trying to know what makes the Lord so mean and visit these trials on Flora and me. Every year I sells something else till now there is nothing left except the floors and the walls—and they is not going to last much longer, either.' He could not see the restless men now or hear their muttering. He peered out to where sea stacs of weird shape lay off the island to the south-west. 'But even allowing for all that I am not for giving up and leaving. I consider the dear Lord must have let things go as bad they can get by this time. Us poor crofters can expect Him to start showering His blessings on us just any day now.'

Before he could say another word the first man who had cried out against him looked around his fellows as if to rally them.

'The dear Lord has had plenty time to shower us over with this glorious treasure Cruachan is shouting about,' he said in a sarcastic voice. 'I'm not for giving the Lord any more time. If these Government men asks me if I wants to leave this island I'm for telling them yes.'

'And so will I,' said another, a tall spare man who stood with the collar of his long black coat turned up around his face as if he had been ill and could not face the slight, damp wind now coming in across the bay. 'Cruachan Campbell talks there about the Lord as if He was maybe going to turn us all into bally toffs tomorrow. I loves the Lord like any other man, but I don't think He is going to do a thing for any of us here on this island. Them men can have my name for moving.'

'Let's see them Government men now!' roared another. 'There is no time like now for telling them men we want to leave.'

Cruachan stood on the jetty against the fading light with the dead hope lying in his chest like a physical weakness. 'By Hell, them Government men will do you just no bit of good at all,' he said weakly. 'People from over the water there is only out to cheat us poor people in the islands.'

But so high were their voices raised that no one heard him. Some had started to walk in the direction taken by the officials. They hurried as if afraid that they were missing something.

'Don't go,' Cruachan said. 'I know them kind of men. By Hell, you just cannot trust men like that, at all! The dear Lord and me know they will only cheat you.'

'You and the dear Lord will be the death of each other yet, so you will!' one of the men shouted. 'You Campbells is the queerest people on this whole island. Sometimes you Campbells just does not seem like real human people at all. You does not seem to want to improve yourself, any way. The rest of us men wants to go some place where a man can put his seeds in the ground and then sit down on the wall and light his pipe and watch them come up into the sun, strong and straight like they should be, not drowneded in that old peat.'

Cruachan shook his head at the man. 'By Goddy, us Campbells is real human people, all right, and don't you go saying we is not! The dear Lord would not like you saying that about me.' He tried to wave an arm, but all at once it was as if his sleeve had been filled with rock. As Cruachan shouted, the men moved slowly away. But one man who had several times shouted jeeringly at Cruachan seemed still to have something to say. 'We would all have been away long ago to some better place and settled down, too, if you had signed that bloody petition!' he shouted angrily. 'All your talk about building a lazybed and growing potatoes has kept us all with empty bellies and no money when we could have been away.'

His resentment seemed to mount into rage. He stood alone on the beach, pointing accusingly across the pebbles at Cruachan's motionless figure. 'I'm warning you, Cruachan Campbell. Don't hold us up no more or it will be the worse for you.'

He suddenly darted at a pebble, lifted it and hurled it at Cruachan. It struck the centre of his brow, the force of it jarring through to the bone and the sharp edge piercing his skin. The man who had thrown the pebble stood dumbly on the beach as he saw the first black gush of blood flowing down Cruachan's forehead. Astonishment at what he had done kept him there until he saw Cruachan's hand rise to brush the blood from his eyes. Then, as if released by this movement, he turned like a startled beast and fled.

The others, too, seeing that Cruachan did not fall, turned and hurried on, desperate to be away.

Through the haze Cruachan saw them go.

'You did not have to go and do this to me,' he whispered. 'I was only wanting to warn you about them cheats from over there.'

13

DECEMBER 24th, and the island white with snow.

'By Goddy,' Cruachan said to Flora when he rose at daylight, 'it is just like Christmas, right enough! Snow certainly is one of the nicest things the dear Lord makes.'

He came away from the window and raked the ash that was still red from the previous night. Then he went out to get a bucket of peat. When he came back Flora was coming out of Our Sheena's room.

'She's away!' she said excitedly. 'She's no' anywhere in the house.'

'Who is away?' Cruachan asked, looking energetically about the room.

'Our Sheena's gone. I've looked everywhere. She must have been away afore we got up.'

In the wastes of Flora's breast a sense of real concern suddenly blossomed. She knew that Our Sheena's baby could be born at any time. 'Ye'll have to go and get the doctor,' she said urgently. 'Something's happened. Dr. Munro will know what to do. He's supposed to be coming, anyway, but we'd better make sure. Quick! Away an' get him.'

Cruachan recoiled from the thought of trudging through the snow to the bonfire. 'By Hell, I just don't know at all what's happening!' he complained. 'Our Sheena has picked the day she is having a baby to go and get lost in the snow. That girl should be right there in her bed and the dear Lord knows that is true.'

'We all know it's true, well enough, ye silly old clown, but the girl hasna been right in the head for months, babbling away about visions and angels. Something's happened to her and we'd better get the doctor here.'

When Cruachan at last departed, Flora and Mairi Fiona walked to the nearest house at the other end of the Bay of the Angels, but no one there had seen Our Sheena. The early Christmas Eve dusk was down when, some three hours later, Cruachan and Dr. Munro came crunching over the snow. Flora was at the open door, staring outwards. Her whole physical appearance seemed to have softened.

The doctor looked anxious. 'Any news, Mrs. Campbell?'

Flora shook her head.

'What on earth can have happened to her? The girl's due any time now. She should be warm in the house in weather like this. We've got to find her soon.' His face was grave as he went into the house and stood by the lamp. 'Is there nothing she said recently that would give us any idea where to look for her?'

They shook their heads.

'Are you sure she didn't leave any message, then? Have you looked in her room?' He reached up and took the lamp from its hook. 'Let's have a look again. You never know.'

The blankets were still lying over the foot of the bed where Our Sheena had thrown them. Her bonnet lay on a chair at the side of the bed and beside it her bible.

'She's done nothing but read that bible day an' night since she came home,' Flora said. 'She must've been in a right state when she left or she'd have taken it with her.'

The doctor lifted the battered book from the chair and held it to the glow of the lamp. It was open at the second chapter of St. Luke and there was a pencil-mark against verse vii, as if Our Sheena had considered the words there to be of more than ordinary significance. The old man's voice sounded almost unbearably solemn in the small room as he read:

114

' "And she brought forth her first-born son, and wrapped him in swaddling clothes, and laid him in a manger, because there was no room for them in the inn." '

Flora and Cruachan listened blankly. But to the doctor it was as if the words were indeed a divine revelation declaring to him across the ages the madness that was in Our Sheena's head. 'The poor girl must be mad if she's done what I think she has,' he said in a hushed voice. 'All this religion's gone to her head.'

He held the book under the lamp again. Farther down the page there was another pencil-mark. Again he read in the same rapt voice: ' "For unto you is born this day in the city of David, a Saviour, which is Christ the Lord. And this shall be a sign unto you: Ye shall find the babe wrapped in swaddling clothes, lying in a manger." '

He threw the bible on to the bed with a thump. Then he seized Cruachan by the arm and shook him. 'Man, man,' he said, 'that poor big girl of yours must be out her mind! This is what she was talking about when she told her mother about the angel. Dear God, we've got to find the poor child quickly or Heaven knows what will happen to her in this terrible weather. It's freezing out there and unless it's me that's gone mad Our Sheena is lying in some old byre or stable and as like as not, at this very minute, crying out for her mother, or the mercy of God.'

On the doctor's instructions Cruachan tied two blankets together and slung them over his shoulder. Then, with Flora insisting on accompanying them, they left the tin house.

It had started to snow again, lightly, with the flakes drifting soundlessly through the still night and the navigation light on Erray Rock blinking at them over the water. It was Dr. Munro's plan that they should get help from the scattering of houses at the other end of the bay, and by the yellow, guiding light of his ancient lantern they hurried along the track. It was wet and treacherous from the snow that had thawed on it throughout the day. Several times

Cruachan slipped and fell. Flora's breath came in painful gasps. Only the slim and wiry doctor seemed to manage without strain. After they had gone almost a quarter of a mile he stopped and pointed through the falling snow to where a light had appeared.

'It's coming towards us,' he said. 'Let's hope it's her!'

They hurried on, and a minute or two later met a figure almost completely covered in snow. It was old Calum Campbell, Cruachan's cousin, from the house in the centre of the island to which Our Sheena had made her mysterious visit a few weeks earlier.

'Thank God it is you!' he gasped, as he recognized them. 'That big girl of yours is lying in my old stable and by the looks of it she is having a baby right there in the straw.'

He brushed the snow from his eyes. 'A baby right there in the srraw,' he repeated.

Dr. Munro grasped him by the arm. 'Is she all right?'

'I don't know about that, Doctor, at all. She was crying out loud enough to frighten me. It was the cries of her that made me find her when I was out to get some peats. I think she must be raving with all the pain that's on her. She said she did not want a doctor. She said Mary did not have a doctor, whatever that means.'

Flora stood with her face fixed in its old inscrutable pattern, saying nothing, asking nothing, waiting only to move on. Echoes of her own sufferings in childbirth came to her out of the general agony of the last thirty years. The memories united her with her daughter in a way that even the previous day would have been impossible.

It was another half-hour before they reached the sheltered cluster of Calum's house and steading. Flora and the doctor went quickly into the shadowy old stable, but Cruachan, after one frightened look round the door, retreated to the house with his cousin.

The place where Our Sheena had chosen to lie was a dilapidated stone building dating from the days when Calum Campbell had kept a horse which he hired out at ploughing time to the other islanders. Dampness glistened on the rough walls, and through a hole in a corner of the roof snow fell down past the grimy rafters and dusty cobwebs to the wet cobblestone floor. The air was strong with the smell of straw, old dung and rotting wood.

Our Sheena lay in a corner, protected from the floor by only a thin layer of mildewed straw. Her hands were thrust out behind her, grasping a rusty iron tethering ring embedded in the wall above her head. She looked like an ill-treated prisoner manacled to the wall of a medieval dungeon. Crouching on the floor beside the girl's twisting body, trying to assist and support her, was Calum's wife. As they entered, a sound of relief came from the old woman. 'Thank God you've got here, Doctor!' she sobbed. 'I don't think I could bear another minute on my own watching the sore pain this poor lass is in. I've done what I could, but it's a doctor the poor thing needs. There's something terrible far wrong.'

The doctor interrupted her. 'How long has she been like this?'

'Oh, I don't know, Doctor. A long time. It's a mercy you've arrived, for if this goes on it'll kill her.'

As she spoke, a cry came from Our Sheena. The fingers of her great hands clenched like pythons round the ring to which the horse had once been tied and her long arms stretched taut in a fierce effort to ease her pain. Again and again the cry was torn from her as if in one agonizing night she was being repaid for the sins of her whole life. Her great arms strained until it seemed that the iron fixture must either be torn from the wall or the whole side of the stable itself be rent and her suffering ended in a deluge of masonry.

In the seconds that had passed since he and Flora arrived, Dr. Munro had thrown off his pack and found the equipment he needed. Now he knelt on the cobbles beside Our Sheena.

'For God's sake help her, Doctor!' Flora sobbed. She went down beside him on the filthy floor and wiped the sweat from the girl's face.

As the doctor gave her the anaesthetic, Our Sheena's tormented body became quiet. Rats scraped and scurried in the empty manger. Old Mrs. Campbell stumbled through the snow with basins of hot water from the house. Flora retreated to a shadowy position by the rattling and shuddering door. She stood there with her arms folded tightly in front of her as if she were clutching something—some memory. The snow drifted down through the hole in the roof, falling unheeded on her hair and on the black shawl that she wore instead of a coat. Suddenly she began to croon. She crooned as if for someone already dead. It was a wailing, keening sound born somewhere in the island's tragic history. As the gruesome strains of the old burial song struck through the silence of the stable, Dr. Munro sprang to his feet.

'Stop it, woman! Stop it or get out!' he shouted.

Flora went silent. Then, from the darkness, there came the sound of her weeping.

The baby when it came was silent and still.

When he could leave Our Sheena the doctor turned to the small body lying limp and quiet on the straw. Fiercely he toiled at it. He tried to breathe life down into the small lungs, to arouse some stirring by massaging the thin white chest. Then, in a last desperate effort to galvanize it with life he thrust it into the mound of snow at Flora's feet.

Nothing happened.

As he turned hopelessly round he saw Our Sheena watching him. She was newly conscious and in the mild light of the lantern she was almost beautiful, like a tall tree in early springtime. She held out her hands for the baby.

The doctor shook his head. 'Lie still, lass,' he said. 'We'll get you out of here in a minute or two. But just now, just you lie still.'

Gently he put the lifeless body down.

118

'Emmanuel! Emmanuel!' The girl's cry came thin and despairing. It trembled for a moment over the small, still form in the straw and then rose upwards through the blackness and the snow of the Christmas night.

14

FOR a day or two a thin suggestion of spring had been engaging Cruachan. No one else had noticed it yet, but to him the signs were all there—a tremor of the air, a swiftness about the birds, a rustling, almost, in the earth itself. Later, others would see such obvious things as a sprouting bush or a shaft of hot sunlight.

January had passed quietly in the tin house. An emotional truce had fallen on the family during Our Sheena's slow return to health. For more than a week following the loss of her baby the girl lay at such a depth of emptiness that there were days when it seemed that she might die. The loss not only of her child, but of her mad dream, had combined into a bereavement of such immensity that Dr. Munro made the long journey from Linga every day. But at last the dullness began to leave her eyes and by the third week of the month she was eating with interest the delicacies that the doctor brought from his own kitchen.

Now, in the second week of February, she had rejoined the household.

Flora, now that the crisis was over, had lapsed back into girning normality.

What now filled Cruachan was a determination that this year he would build his lazybed. He could sense, in the faint unfoldings of spring, that the time when he would surge into activity was near. But not just yet. Not today. Perhaps tomorrow. . . .

He had finished his porridge and was about to go out and look for a likely place to start digging when Sandy McCaskill arrived with the two officials who had visited the island in December. To Cruachan they were figures of doom, and he was shocked and resentful that McCaskill should bring them to his house. It was McCaskill who had to find the men a chair as Cruachan stood awkwardly in front of the fire, awed and afraid, despite himself.

'Well, Cruachan, man,' said McCaskill, 'I've brought these two gentlemen to have a wee word with you, but maybe I had better tell you first what has been happening.' He stopped. He seemed embarrassed. 'It's that thing you said they would never do, Cruachan, the evacuation. Well, they're offering to do it now. Everybody that wants to can go. They're going to sail us over to the mainland in two lots. It is a great chance for us all, Cruachan, and they want you and Flora and the girls to come too.'

Cruachan heard the words as if they came through some muffling obstruction. He stood quite stiff and still by the fire, looking past McCaskill, through the grimy window to where the sun was shining on a patch of faded green grass. He could see the dew glistening on it like tears; his own tears.

'That's right, Mr. Campbell,' one of the officials said. 'What Mr. McCaskill says is true. The Minister has decided that Torrismore is economically untenable. A place at Lochamorven in Argyll has been chosen for re-settling the whole island population so that you can continue to live as a community.'

The voice went on. Houses would be provided. There was a village, a railway station, a bus service.

'Not like here,' said the man, 'where there's nothing.'

'Nothing?' Cruachan said, seizing the word. 'By Hell, I wouldn't call this old island nothing! No, by God! Not nothing! All we need here is time to get the land into shape and a good cheap boat service to take the things we grow and bring in the things we need. That's all this old island needs. I just don't know what you mean by nothing. By Hell, I don't!'

The official who had not yet spoken smiled persuasively. 'I can well understand that this is your home and you feel attached to it, Mr. Campbell. But think of your wife and family. Wouldn't they like a nice modern house and shops to go to and a big town like Oban only a few miles away?'

'My wife and daughters do not give a damnation about bally shops,' Cruachan said in a rising voice. 'But what you said about a nice house is right enough. Women like a nice house. That's why I'm busy doing that very thing—building a new house. It's right out there, just across the croft, and just as soon as I can get that big brick house finished we're going to move straight into it out this old tin house.'

'Well, if we can't persuade you, Mr. Campbell, we had better make the position perfectly clear,' one of the officials said at last. 'I have a list here of every man, woman and child on Torrismore. Other than the members of your own household, they are all re-signed to the fact that they must leave here and have signed several petitions asking this to be undertaken by the Government. The plan is that half the present population will be removed on a special steamer with all their belongings at the end of April or beginning of May. The remainder will be evacuated at the end of the summer when the work of preparing accommodation for them at Locha-morven will have been completed. When they go you and your family will be the sole inhabitants of Torrismore. The present mail-boat service will doubtless be withdrawn, as there would obviously be insufficient inducement for the proprietors to continue it. That means you will be dependent for mail and all supplies on the next nearest island, Linga. You will be even more isolated than now. Do you understand that?'

'By Hell, if all the other folk on this island is the kind that wants to leave, then I consider we will get on better without them!'

Cruachan said. He was glowering sullenly. To every problem Cruachan had the answer and his determination was unshaken when the men rose at last to go.

'You're the bloodiest, stubbornest man I've ever heard of, Cruachan Campbell,' McCaskill said, as they reached the sunlight of the rough grass. 'How the bally Hell you think you Campbells can go on living here if every other man and woman leaves I just do not know.'

Suddenly he pointed across the croft at the sagging outline of the brick house. 'That bally old falling-down stack o' bricks hanging by a thread is the wonderful house he's been raving about,' he said to the embarrassed visitors. 'You would think it was a great big mansion fit for the gentry to live in to hear him. But that's it there. Creaking and almost tottering in the breeze, it is, and never a damn' bit o' work done on it for years. It's been standing there like that since I was a laddie and used to come round here to have a laugh at the house that Cruachan Campbell built. And it'll never be finished. They'll never live in it.' His anger seemed almost to be choking him. 'Man, man,' he cried, turning on Cruachan, 'even the rats are not safe there in that house you've stuck together with sand for mortar and never a beam or a timber where it's needed!'

Cruachan could endure the years of want, the grip of hunger, all the barbs that accompanied his poverty, but this assault on the creation of his heart could not be borne.

'Holy Jesus, you should be dead and in your grave for saying that, Sandy McCaskill!' he shouted in a broken voice. 'That is the wickedest thing a man ever said and the dear Lord will strike you down for it. That big house I'm building over there is beautiful. It's beautiful like the sun lighting up the waves or the sound of a burn running down the mountain, or the smell of bog myrtle blowing over the land at night.' His throat was aching. Fumblingly he searched for some further praise. 'By Hell, to me and any other man with an eye to see it that big house is like a prayer, the way it

123

goes reaching up there into the sky, right up to where God Himself is!'

He turned to the two officials as if there he might find support, but all he saw was the discomfort of men accustomed to a society in which emotion of this crude variety was decently concealed. Their silence inflamed him, implying, as it did, agreement with the postmaster.

'The dear Lord knows I never asked any of you people to come and see me here!' he shouted. 'You people have pushed yourself in here where you is not wanted. Now, by Hell, if you don't get off this tin house croft bally quick I just don't know what I'll do! This is my place and I don't want people like you on it at all.'

For hours after they had gone Cruachan sat morosely by the fire. The news that the island was to be abandoned at last was lost in the greater feeling unleashed by McCaskill's reviling of the big brick house. Cruachan had been vaguely aware of the passing years and the lack of progress made with the house. But somehow he had never imagined that anyone else would notice. He remembered hearing once that a cathedral with a name like *Notterdam* had taken six hundred years to complete. It, of course, had been constructed by foreigners, who were notoriously lazy, but it was an indication that a house meant for God could not be completed in just a day. He cursed his failure to remember this crushing fact when McCaskill had been talking his bally blethers.

Despite the comforting recollection, however, there grew steadily in him a terrible yearning to find some means of finishing the big brick house. His pride, which seemed at times to have died, was booming out. If McCaskill could make the statements that he had, then what might other people be saying? Cruachan did not care so much for himself. What he could not bear was the idea of the house that he was making for God being defiled by vulgar laughter. To tolerate that, to allow it to go on, would be an unforgivable sin.

While he toiled at the problem, sickening himself with remorse, there came back to him words spoken by Murdo Mhor.

'*If ever you needs any help, just you let me know, Cruachan. Murdo Mhor is not the man to forget his friends.*'

That was what the money-lender had said. Suddenly it seemed to him that Murdo Mhor might be the instrument that God had chosen to help him finish the big brick house. The idea thumped in his brain. Purposefully, he got to his feet. He would do the thing he had always refused to do. He would ask Murdo Mhor to lend him money. Not, as other people did, for mere earthly comforts, but for the lofty purpose of buying enough bricks to finish the house that was for God.

Murdo Mhor welcomed him with the intent look of a man who has collected every known butterfly but one and now realizes that the elusive survivor may at last be about to flutter into his net. 'Come away in and we'll just have a wee dram of the *White Hearse* and talk it over, then, whatever it is,' he said, guiding Cruachan to a fireside chair.

Flora was lighting the lamp when Cruachan came into the house, his eyes bright with whisky. Behind him hovered the furtive shape of the money-lender. Cruachan's voice was unusually authoritative. 'Where's Mairi Fiona?' he asked. 'I wants Mairi Fiona. Is she in?'

'What d'ye want her for?' Flora asked obstructively. 'Ye should be ashamed to let anybody see ye in a state like that, let alone your own daughter.'

As they stood glowering at each other, the door from the kitchen porch creaked slowly open and Mairi Fiona appeared carrying a stack of plates, saucers and cups for the tea-table. At the sight of Murdo Mhor she cowered back and tried to leave. But Cruachan had seen her. 'Don't go running away now, Mairi Fiona,' he commanded. 'Your daddy wants to see you.' He gripped her by the shoulder and pushed her to the centre of the room where she stood under the lamp with the crockery rattling in her arms. 'I've got a wee surprise for you,' he said. He bent over her confidingly. 'You know how poor your mammy and me is, Mairi Fiona, with just this old tin house above our heads and hardly a thing in our bellies? Well, your Uncle Murdo Mhor has a vacancy on his household staff and because he's such a good friend of your daddy's he is going to appoint you to the situation.'

Flora had endured all up to now, but this staggering revelation made her cry out in disgust.

'Ye rotten auld faggot!' she snarled across the table. 'Ye're so full o' whisky ye don't know what ye're saying.'

'By Hell, I knows what I'm saying, all right, and I does not want any interfering from you!' Cruachan replied. His back was very straight and his voice strong. He was feeling for the first time in decades the mad surge of success. He was going to get the bricks at last. The cost hardly seemed to matter.

Murdo Mhor had led him on, filling his glass, bringing out a decrepit ledger and writing down the number of bricks needed like a commercial traveller gratefully receiving an order. And all the time he was remembering Cruachan's spittle on his boots. Not until the very end had he named the price. Cruachan's decision was taken without any active consent from him. Somewhere in a corner of his mind the place that Roddy lived had started to open—like a crypt—ready to receive Mairi Fiona.

Now, as Flora faced him across the table, he was unshakable.

'Ye're rotten wi' drink!' Flora cried. 'Ye're mirac'lous. It's not so very long ago that ye were threatening to do in that dirty big midden that's hiding there behind ye. Now ye're drooling ower him. Now he's Uncle Murdo Mhor. Well, uncle or no uncle, Mairi Fiona's not going anywhere near his house again. Ye know what happened the last time she set foot in it.'

Cruachan was ready for anything. 'Nothing at all happened,' he said. The extraordinary processes of mind that had protected him for so long had smoothed the way once more. 'Murdo Mhor has explained all that to me, so he has. It was just a mistake. That's all it was—a mistake, and the dear Lord knows that. Mairi Fiona was just excited and imagining things the way you bally women are always doing.'

The money-lender spoke for the first time. 'That's right now, Flora. It was just a terrible big mistake like I said it was at the time. You know I wouldn't do anything like that, and me in business here. Anyway, it would be an awful thing to do that thing Mairi Fiona said I did.'

A sob from Mairi Fiona, who stood shrinking at her mother's side, followed this almost mocking declaration. 'Oh, Mammy, I don't want to go,' she said. 'I want to stay here. I'm frightened of that man.'

Cruachan was like an addict within sight of an enslaving drug. 'By Hell, stop that bally noise, Mairi Fiona, or I will give you something to shout about!' he ranted, leaning threateningly over the table. 'I'm your daddy, so I am, and I certainly would not put you anywhere that was not nice. You're a big girl now and, by Goddy, it is bally high time you were earning your mammy and me some money!' He gave her what was meant to be a reassuring push. 'Now stop your silly crying and away and get your things parcelled up. It is not to Timbuktu you are going to, but only a mile away from the tin house. You can see your mammy and daddy any time you likes, and you will only be away just a month or two, anyway'—his face suddenly shaded over with an angry memory—'for, by Hell, come this summer there will be no Murdo Mhor or anybody else left on this island but us Campbells!'

Flora had retreated. She was sheltering now in the secret place that she had found early in her marriage and to which she had fled ten thousand times.

They gathered for a moment on the grass outside the house, then the money-lender and Mairi Fiona walked away.

As soon as he judged the disappearing figures to be out of hearing, Cruachan turned eagerly to Flora. 'Murdo Mhor is going to get me all the stuff I needs to finish off the big brick house,' he said. He was like a boy who has been keeping a secret with difficulty. 'The next mail-boat out of here will be taking a letter to Glasgow ordering up the biggest heap of bricks. I can hear them already, tumbling off the puffer on to the beach like the sound of the waves with a south-west gale behind.'

Flora made no move or sound.

'By Hell, is there no way at all I can make you smile, Flora?' Cruachan said. 'Can you hear me? Do you not know what I am saying to you? We will be out of this old tin house and into that big real brick house I'm building in just a month or two. And we will have Mairi Fiona back with us, too.'

Flora turned to him. Her voice was queer. 'If ye ever get that house finished or live in it, Cruachan Campbell, I'll ken for certain that there's no God.'

15

GRAMPA CAMPBELL crouched at a crack in the door of his room and squinted through. The rest of the family were getting ready for the mission hall. Abrach was back on Torrismore and would be preaching at noon. Grampa was impatient for them all to get out of the house. He had plans of his own for that Sunday morning.

Now, more than ever, he was the family outcast. Roddy had always had a talk with him in the evenings. Even Mairi Fiona, despite her idiotic giggling, had been a *divertissement* in his lonely isolation. Now these two were gone, and the three remaining occupants of the tin house ignored him. All Grampa had now was his beloved coffin and his unconquerable stomach. It was his unemployed gastric juices that were energizing him now, keeping him bent to his spy-hole at the door, filling his old frame with a fretful wish to see the three of them gone so that he might get on with his own project. Every year at this time the old man stretched his rations by collecting gulls' eggs from the colony of nests on the shelves of the mountainside.

With a mutter of relief, he saw Cruachan go out the front door, followed by Flora and the looming figure of Our Sheena. Grampa took his watery eye from the door and scurried over to the bedpost to get his cap. Then, twitching with expectancy, he went out of the house. The others had just rounded the dry-stone wall and were walking along the track. Grampa shuffled behind them for a short way, then stepped off the track and disappeared among the boulders.

It was so long since the old man had been to the mission hall that no one ever thought now to ask him. Grampa did not, in any case, believe much in missionaries or in mission halls. Grampa believed in death and in the rumblings of his empty stomach and it was his custom to refer to the Campbell family's procession to the mission hall as *the hens' march to the midden*.

For an hour he gorged himself on raw eggs, stuffing them madly into his mouth like a greedy child with sweets. As he crawled breathlessly about the narrow ledges, he was followed by the mournful cries of the birds. He moved from nest to nest, heedless of their distress. His craving was insatiable. His appetite increased the more he took, like a drunkard with whisky.

Pitilessly, he crashed through the nests when there was no other way for him to go. Entire nests were dislodged and slithered down the rocky slopes. The old man's clothes were blotched with the yolks of shattered eggs. He was like a murderer stained by the blood of his crime. The crazed birds cried hysterically and then, as he moved on, circled dementedly over the ruins. There was no flicker of sympathy in Grampa Campbell as he left them mourning. This was what the island and God had made of him. At last he came to rest. His bones ached with the strain of his frenzied exertions. Only now that he had stopped his fierce feeding did he feel the pain in his old, ill-used and overloaded body. He was limp; almost comatose. He felt almost as if he had solidified inside. He rose dazedly to his feet, wondering if there were perhaps a nest nearby from which he could snatch one last mouthful. His empty legs trembled and the ragged ends of his trousers flapped in the breeze. He looked like some grotesque seaside comedian who had been pelted with eggs.

Along the mountainside a lone gull flapped a plaintive way. As he turned, Grampa saw the big bird's approach. Although it was at least a hundred yards away, and higher, his befuddled senses cried a warning. He recoiled, throwing up his arms as if he were being attacked. For a moment he swayed in a crouching position as the bird passed harmlessly overhead. Shakily, he straightened, his tottery old feet moving aimlessly on the rocky platform. Then, as if pushed, he stepped forward and went over the edge.

Cruachan, Flora and Our Sheena were on the track below, plodding homeward. They heard, from somewhere ahead, and hidden to them, Grampa's cry. Then the clatter of rolling rock and the sound of scree slithering down the crags and falling dryly from one ledge to the next.

'By Hell, that sounds like somebody falling down the mountain!' Cruachan said. He ran forward and round a bend in the track.

When Flora and Our Sheena turned the corner they saw him kneeling beside the body. Scree was still dripping from the ledges of rock like a small, gritty waterfall.

'It is all right,' Cruachan shouted. 'It is only Grampa.'

The old man was lying across the track, face downwards. One of his boots had been dragged off and had landed in the water. It was now floating out to sea on the receding tide like a small black boat, the lace still tied in a tight bow at the side. Grampa's egg-stained jacket had been swept upwards by the violent rush of air as he fell and it now covered his downcast head like a shabby shroud.

'Is he dead?' Flora asked. She was awed, but unexcited.

Cruachan lifted back the jacket. His father's eyes were shut and his head was turned down into his chest at a curious angle. He had fallen more than one hundred feet. 'By Hell, you just can't turn round or even go to the mission hall without Grampa doing some mischief!' Cruachan said. 'If Grampa is not stealing our food then he is knocking about and breaking things. Now he's gone and fell off the mountain.' He shook his head. 'Can you beat it? A man this age climbing up the crags like a goat for gulls' eggs and him so well fed at the tin house.'

Our Sheena was bent almost double in her effort to see. 'Is he dead?' she asked.

Cruachan did not hear her. He was kneeling on the track, his face narrowed into a curious expression. His hands were going through his father's pockets. Just when it looked as if he might not find anything, he pulled two eggs from a pocket of the jacket. 'Well, if this is not the funniest thing,' he said, like a collector pointing out something of real interest. 'Grampa is all smashed up and these two eggs has not even a chip.' He shook the eggs at his ear. 'These gulls' eggs make a brave bit of eating, right enough, though I just can't remember when I last ate one.'

He cracked one of the eggs between his fingers and, tilting his head back, dropped the contents into his mouth. Flora and Our Sheena glowered. They both liked gulls' eggs as much as Cruachan.

'How many o' them eggs did ye get off Grampa, ye greedy auld thing?' Flora asked. 'We like gulls' eggs as well as you.'

'There was only two,' said Cruachan, and before either of them could stop him he dropped the other down his throat.

'You must be the greediest man ever, Daddy,' Our Sheena said.

Cruachan ignored this and crawled over the grass to where Grampa's checked cap lay. He pulled it on, tugging it into the shape of his head.

'That jacket looks as if it would be a fit for ye as well,' Flora said. She was like a woman at a bargain counter.

Our Sheena was staring sternly at the still bundle. 'Any man that goes climbing for eggs in defiance of the Lord's Holy Sabbath Day has no good in him at all,' she said. 'The dear Lord has cast Grampa off that ledge up there in His terrible wrath at the Sabbath being broken. This is what Abrach and me has been warning all you sinners about. You just can't meddle about with the Lord like Grampa did, climbing for eggs on the Sabbath. That's what the Holy Bible is all about.'

132

'Praise the Lord,' Cruachan said. He bent down and put his hands under his father's shoulders. 'Take Grampa's legs,' he said.

Flora took one leg. For a moment it looked as if Our Sheena might refuse to touch the other sinful limb; then, as if remembering some obscure scriptural authority that made the handling of an irreligious corpse permissible, she bent and did as bidden.

Grampa's head shook loosely about as they carried him back to the tin house. They put him on his bed in the cold back room and left him there.

It was dark when Abrach returned to the tin house. When Cruachan told him about Grampa he pursed his lips, shook his head and said: 'What else could the dear Lord do when faced wi' such wickedness? If I was the Lord I'd have done the self-same thing. Sabbath-breaking is a filthy abomination that neither me or the Lord is standing for.'

Abrach's return to the island had coincided with a big change in Our Sheena. All the listlessness and guilt that had hung about her since her illness suddenly disappeared. Now, whenever Abrach was near, she was like a reformed drunkard confronted with an open bottle. Our Sheena was constantly filled with a desire both to enfold Abrach like a mother and to devour him. The emotion that she felt for him was the same blinding confusion raised in her by the thought of God. It was a passion that ran from the fierce to the flippant; a flame that, however it might flicker, was never extinguished. Now she watched Abrach from her chair at the table— silent, but filled with the old wish.

A small evening breeze with rain behind it was rattling one of the corrugated sections at the back of the house, but no one seemed to notice it.

Cruachan rose stiffly to his feet and walked out to the grass. For a long time he stood motionless, peering into the blackness like a man admiring a distant view. He could feel the stirrings of the new season in all directions. He could feel it in the softness of the damp wind on his face, and in a dozen rustlings and squeakings in the night. It came to him in the scent of things beginning to grow again and in the smell somewhere of a crofter burning the old grass and heather to get the earth ready for the work of another year—forgetful that he would be gone before the harvest. All these things Cruachan felt. And they hurt him. They hurt him because they raised longings that the nature of the earth and the economics of the day would not allow him to fulfil. He stood alone in the darkness —rising out of the earth like the mountain and the whinstone Angels behind him—until the night air had him shivering. Only then did he return to the house.

Flora was in bed and asleep. A droning sound, like a choir of monks reciting a litany, was coming from Grampa's room. It was a sound that Cruachan knew well: the sound of Abrach praying for purification. As he listened, the drone of supplication rose to a wailing note, and then, after a few tense seconds, sank to an odd moaning.

Every Sunday night, wherever he was, Abrach observed the same ritual. It was one of his beliefs that he took upon himself the sins of those he prayed for and that during his hectic Sabbath preaching he became heavily contaminated by the sins of the congregation. Before getting into bed he always got down on the floor and prayed for the black burden to be lifted. He saw himself as engaged in a fierce struggle with the devil, and often ended up writhing on the floor as if in real physical combat.

'By Hell, Abrach certainly is having a right stiff do with the bally devil this night!' Cruachan said, as the moaning from the back room increased not only in volume but in the quality of feeling that was in it. It was the sound of a man beset, and yet finding relief.

The noise was having a strange effect on Our Sheena. She had risen to her knees from her sitting position on the floor at the side of the hearth. Her eyes were bright and her body leaned forward. She was as alert and ready for movement as a snake.

The turmoil in the back room rose to a new intensity, quickly followed by an outbreak of thumping, as if the missionary had started beating his hands on the walls. Our Sheena sprang from the floor and crossed the room. 'Abrach is in need of some help to fight the devil,' she said. 'I can tell.' She wrenched the door open and went into the darkness of the back room before Cruachan could say a word.

In the startled instant in which he saw her outlined against the lamplight of the other room, Abrach fell silent and lay still upon the floor.

Our Sheena could hear him breathing but she could not see him. 'The Lord has sent me to help you drive away the devil, Abrach,' she whispered. 'The dear Lord has just told me that He wants for us to drive out the devil, the two of us like one.' As she spoke, she threw off her uniform jacket. Abrach made no reply, but as he heard the sound of her clothes being thrown about he began to breath like a trapped animal.

'The dear Lord sent me a message to come and help you, Abrach. Us lady missionaries has ways of soothing the devil right out of a man as nice as anything.'

Our Sheena spoke like a mother to a child, but Abrach did not answer. He could feel sin in the room, repelling and luring him. With his heart he wanted to run and go crashing through the door. But something else in him—the part of him that he had denied all his life, crying, sometimes, with the pain of it—pinned him where he was, holding him in the beam of erotic energy that Our Sheena was casting about the room like a searchlight's ray. He was appalled and yet eager; deserted, it seemed, by the iron self-denial that had sustained him for so long.

Our Sheena stared about the room, her eyes fighting to defeat the blackness. She stretched out her long bare arms, but all she touched was the bed on which Grampa lay. She swung in another direction. 'Where is you, Abrach?' Her voice was pleading. 'You know we has to pitch out the devil like one now. The dear Lord has just told me so.'

Silence.

No answering voice.

'Reach out your lovely hand to me, sweet Abrach, so we can start to pray together like one. Why are you so quiet there in the dark, my Abrach? Put out your dear hand, now, like the Lord says you should.'

She crouched by the door and began to hum one of the Assembly's hymn-tunes. It was an elemental sound, like the early stirrings of a storm. Abrach shivered. His voice did not rise to join with hers. Our Sheena could wait no longer. She began to creep across the floor, her hands stretched out for the missionary as she went.

From under the boarded-up window there came a scuffling noise as Abrach tried to shrink farther away. 'It's no' what the Lord likes at all,' he sobbed. 'It's a thing I've never done before.'

It was all Our Sheena needed. She hurled herself across the room and gathered him up. 'It is what the Lord wants us to do, all right, sweet Abrach,' she sighed in his ear. 'He sent me a message for us to pray like one. Where are your lovely lips, my angel?'

The touch of her had knocked him into squirming silence, but weakly he pushed at her.

'It is what the dear Lord wants, my Abrach,' she whispered, as she carried him across the room and put him down on the bed beside Grampa.

16

CRUACHAN stopped in astonishment, one foot out of the house, the other still inside. He could not believe what he saw. Beyond the litter of boxes and rotting armchairs Abrach and Our Sheena sat together on the grass. To find the two so near was surprising enough, but it was what they were doing that struck Cruachan motionless. Our Sheena had one long arm curled round Abrach's shoulder and her cheek rested gently on his greying hair. The missionary was leaning against the girl, almost like a boy at his mother's side. Somewhere over the wall a small bird sang and the sun sent down a long beam of gentle light that gave the scene a story-book charm.

Although it was happening only a few yards from where he stood, Cruachan could not make himself believe what he saw. He knew that except at times of prayer Abrach shrank even from the touch of Our Sheena's shadow. This must be an hallucination. He knew that this sort of thing could happen to a man if he had been working too hard.

Nevertheless, Cruachan wanted to be sure. He moved his head from one side to the other and stretched his neck like an astonished cat. Then, glancing about to see that he was unobserved, he went down on his knees and crawled for some yards across the grass. He moved with all the caution of a predatory animal, for he did not want to disturb the idyllic pair until he was near enough to see beyond all possible further doubt that they were indeed doing what he was now beginning to think they must be doing.

Our Sheena was still hugging Abrach to her like a woman shopper clutching a valuable parcel. And now across the croft there drifted the soft singing of a hymn-tune. It came from between Our Sheena's wide pink lips. Every few seconds she seemed to be crushing Abrach lovingly to her, and with each clasping her voice rose to a happy squeal. Once, as she stopped singing, she caught one of Abrach's long eyebrows between her white teeth and tugged at it with delicate affection.

Cruachan was less astonished by what he saw Our Sheena doing than by the fact that Abrach did not appear to be protesting. At first he thought the girl was holding the man captive, that she was crushing him so badly that he was unable to call for help. He began to think of possible ways of releasing him. But as he crouched in the grass he was amazed to hear Abrach begin to sing the hymn-tune too.

Cruachan crawled a further few yards in a sideways direction like a crab, and from there he saw that although Abrach's eyes were closed there was a smile on his face. Warily he crept round a wooden box and then onwards, like a soldier under fire, to the cover of one of the armchairs. He was fairly certain now that what he was seeing was actually happening.

For a little longer he watched, then, able to bear the riddle no longer, he bounded across the grass and roughly pushed himself between Our Sheena and Abrach. 'By Hell,' he said, 'this is the funniest way I ever saw two missionaries going on! You and Our Sheena are sitting right here on the grass all wrapped round each other like two bally spiders. I certainly never saw two missionaries doing this before.'

Abrach blushed until he was almost black and Our Sheena giggled. But although she smoothed down her skirt with one demure hand, the girl held tightly to Abrach with the other. Neither of them spoke. Cruachan shook his head in bewilderment and scurried quickly round them again so that he could see just exactly how they were placed.

'What the Hell!' he said, tapping Abrach on the shoulder. 'I consider this is not the way you has been wanting Our Sheena to go on any other time you was staying at the tin house.'

He went round them once more, this time from the opposite direction. 'I just cannot believe, any way at all, it is you two there on the bally grass a-grasping and a-fondling each other like that,' he said.

Our Sheena giggled and pulled Abrach more tightly to her, glancing down at him with a queer intimacy that made Cruachan wonder if they had really been praying all that time in the back room last night. Abrach's face was still red. He could not quite grasp yet that the barriers of the years had gone down in a single night. But he felt that he must explain this staggeringly un-characteristic interlude.

'The dear Lord showed me a real lesson last night when He sent Our Sheena into that back room so that we could fight the devil just like one,' he mumbled. 'The Lord and Our Sheena, both of them thegether, let me see that I just havena been living the way a man was meant to.'

Cruachan rubbed his face and snorted. 'The ways of the dear Lord are queer, right enough, whiles. There is no man at all knows that better nor me, but I will be real surprised if the Lord sent you a bally message you was to fight the devil out here on the grass all wrapped up with Our Sheena, the way you is now.'

Our Sheena was tying knots in the ends of her long fair hair and trying to look as small and bashful as she possibly could. 'Abrach means the Lord has shown him it is all right for him to do now what he had never done before,' she said. 'I showed Abrach in that back room how the dear Lord wants him and me to pray just like one from now on.'

Cruachan looked doubtful. 'It looks to me like you two is just doing what all the other people does without the Lord telling a thing to them,' he muttered. 'It looks to me like you two is just rolling it for each other on the grass there, the way you is all wrapped together so that a man can hardly tell Abrach from Our Sheena.'

Our Sheena looked indignant and reached over to pick up her preaching bonnet. 'There is just no need at all, at all, for you to get excited like that, Daddy,' she said. 'Abrach has got to like us praying and singing like one, as the Lord instructed me to show him last night, and he is now right keen to go on doing it some more.'

'By Hell, Abrach certainly has learned real quick, how to do whatever it is you two is doing!' Cruachan said.

'Nothing takes long once the glorious light o' the Lord shines doon on a man,' Abrach said. He felt that here was firm theological ground on which he could reaffirm his waning authority. 'Saul became Paul quicker than a swallow when the holy light o' our Divine Lord struck him. It was the same in that back room last night.'

'Anyway,' said Our Sheena, 'because Abrach and me is missionaries and good religious people we are proposing to get married and kill the old devil like one from now on, like the dear Lord wants.'

Abrach looked both foolish and apprehensive as he listened to this announcement, like a sobering man hearing of some indiscretion committed in drink. He coughed and rubbed his eyes with the backs of his hands. He felt that in some strange way he had been robbed.

Our Sheena gave him a motherly shake that made his head snap back with a click. 'Isn't that right now, Abrach? Tell Daddy we is to be married.'

'That's what the Lord wants, right enough,' Abrach mumbled, sniggering into his hand. 'He wants us to be like one, though I hadna ever been like one afore last night.'

Flora came shuffling over the grass in her heavy boots, clutching

140

a sickle and a cluster of fresh green nettles that she had been gathering to make soup. Strands of lank hair hung down like straw from under her dust-cap. The sack skirt was tied unevenly round her waist. The ends of the string which held it on to her thin body hung almost to her ankles.

'Abrach and me is getting married!' Our Sheena shouted to her.

Flora came to a halt like a rocking-horse that has lost momentum, but she did not speak.

'That's right,' Abrach said, releasing himself from Our Sheena's grip. 'The Lord wants Our Sheena an' me to be thegether so we can kill the devil easier.'

Flora let the sickle and the nettles fall to the grass. She looked down, almost as if suddenly ashamed, at her disintegrating skirt. Then she produced her empty clay pipe and fitted it into her mouth. Thus equipped, Flora felt more able to probe the strange territory into which she had been so suddenly cast. 'Are ye going to have a real weddin'?' she asked at last. She was thinking of her daughter's previous unsolemnized adventures.

Our Sheena looked shocked. 'Abrach and me are going to be married real, all right,' she said haughtily. 'Abrach and me being missionaries and real children of the Lord are going to marry each the other. Abrach and me are going to marry each the other over there in the mission hall.'

'Are ye going to be one o' them white brides, then?' Flora asked.

Our Sheena sniggered and lowered her eyelids. 'Yes,' she said in a small voice.

Cruachan slapped his legs and danced up and down. 'That certainly is good now!' he shouted. 'Our Sheena is going to be a bride in white.'

'What other colour would there be for a handmaiden o' the Lord the likes o' Our Sheena is?' Abrach asked reprovingly. 'White's the colour that was put aside in Heaven for the pure an' the holy, like missionaries.'

'Praise the Lord,' said Cruachan.

Flora waggled the empty clay pipe up and down in her mouth a few times and then took it out and looked at it with surprise, as if she had not seen it for a very long time and had forgotten what it was.

'Where're you and Abrach going to live?' she asked.

'Everywhere,' said Our Sheena. She stretched out her monumental arms and shook her head so that the long strands of her bright fair hair flew outwards and upwards into the sunshine. 'Abrach and me is going to live everywhere. We is going to travel the islands, going everywhere under the sky that the Lord needs, driving out the devil, like one, wherever we find him.' Gaily she seized Abrach by the hand and pulled him down on to the grass again. 'Isn't that right, Abrach? You and me is going to live everywhere, like two birds in the sky.'

Abrach could only simper.

For a while they stood in the sun. Flora did not speak again. She stood sucking at her empty pipe, retreating back into her private place. Cruachan walked about, judging with his eyes the spot where he would put his lazybed. He still intended, despite the advancing season, despite everything, to raise a crop of potatoes that year.

The tide had turned before someone remembered that they still had Grampa to bury and they went inside the tin house to get him.

17

CRUACHAN looked down at his father's coffin. They had carried it through, empty, from the back room and it lay now on the floor beside the hearth. Every inch of the burnished grain, the elegant hang of the tassels, the smugness of the brass feet, spoke to Cruachan of grandeur—and worth.

As he squatted thoughtfully on his heels and slid his hand over the smooth wood, an uneasy belief that had been rising in him since the previous day formed into a clear conviction. The coffin that he had so often threatened to smash into firewood was clearly an object of value. It was as if he were seeing it for the first time. As he stared down at it a terrible temptation began to fill him. For a moment conscience fluttered through him and then was gone, driven out by his compulsive needs.

From somewhere in a corner of the room he heard Flora complain: 'How long are ye going to stand there looking at it? It's enough to make a body's hair stand on end. The sooner ye get Grampa in there and away the better I'll feel.'

Cruachan crackled stiffly to his feet, rummaging through his pockets for his pipe, but his eyes fixed on the coffin. 'Grampa certainly did do a right fine job on this bally coffin,' he said in an oddly unsteady voice. 'I just don't know at all how I never noticed it before, but now I look at it I consider this is the sweetest old coffin I've ever seen, even better than old Captain Kennedy on Linga had, and him the gentry.' As he spoke, his hand moved over the wood, almost as if, like his father, he was trying to enhance the incomparable gloss. 'Six years at least my daddy worked to make this coffin. There is just no knowing what it would have cost him to buy one even half as bally good as this.'

Flora was trying to chop the nettles without being stung, handling them like scorpions. Abrach and Our Sheena sat silent.

'A man could go to meet the dear Lord feeling right smart wearing this fine coffin Grampa made,' Cruachan said. 'I consider even Matheson over the water there in Oban has not got a coffin near any way as good as this in that funeral shop of his. I consider Matheson would want maybe twelve or fifteen pounds for a coffin with oak wood as smooth as this of Grampa's and a brass plate as shining bright.'

Flora stopped chopping the nettles and looked suspiciously across the room. Our Sheena rose and looked down at the plaque on the coffin lid with its terse inscription—*Gentlemen Lift the Seat*.

'What do them words mean, Daddy?' she asked. 'They are not anything I've ever seen on a coffin lid before. Usually it just says R.I.P. or the name of the dear departed, any funerals I've been at for the Assembly.' She turned to Abrach. 'Do you remember these words anywhere in the Holy Scriptures?'

But Abrach did not know what the words meant, either.

'Maybe they is poetry,' Cruachan said, spitting suddenly on the glittering brass and then bending over to rub it with the sleeve of his jersey. 'Grampa was a real educated man. Anybody can see that from the way he made this coffin.' He looked about him for the first time, holding his head at a curious angle. 'It's funny to think how Grampa never had much money, but if I took this coffin he made to Matheson over in Oban he would pay me ten pounds, as near as anything, for it. Matheson would be right proud to put a coffin as sweet and lovely as this in his window.'

It seemed he could stand still no longer. He started moving round the coffin, adjusting the tassels as if they were not straight and bending down to blow non-existent dust from the brass feet. The clattering of Flora's boots was very loud as she crossed the room and faced him. 'Dear God Almighty,' she said, 'I've never heard the like o't! Ye're nothing but a body-snatcher. I declare to God ye're going to steal that coffin yere auld faither spent years making.'

'By Hell, I was just thinking of you at Our Sheena's marriage ceremony in that bally old sack, Flora!' Cruachan said, looking at the floor. 'I was just thinking if Matheson gave me ten pounds for this nice oak coffin I would get you a real new dress for Our Sheena's marriage ceremony.' He looked suddenly away. 'And I could get me some wood and things I'll be needing to finish off the big brick house once Murdo Mhor gets me them bricks. Next winter we are going to need another house right bad.'

A strange expression had come on Flora's face. She rubbed her skirt, feeling the old, disintegrating material between her fingers. Then she glanced round at the door behind which the old man lay. 'Did Grampa make as good a coffin as would get ten pounds?' she asked.

'By Hell, this coffin my daddy made is so good I consider even some lord or lady would be right pleased to be buried in it!' Cruachan said. 'I can just see how proud Grampa would be up there in Heaven if some lord or lady came up to him and said: "We just came up in that good oak coffin of your make, Grampa, and it was real comfortable." '

Abrach was making choking noises. His hands rose as if to stop Cruachan, but nothing could stop him now.

'Don't you go forgetting, either, Flora, that Grampa never gave us any bally money at all here, not since before Roddy was born. Grampa always did say he would give us money some day for the good food we gave him and the bed he lay down in. Now Grampa has gone and rolled off a ledge and him given us no money at all.' His face was the same as it had been the night he sent Mairi Fiona with Murdo Mhor. His only thought was for the house that had dominated him down the years and which now—with its completion in sight—was directing him down paths that even he had never walked. 'You worked away right hard for Grampa, so you did now, Flora, and Grampa, being the good man he was, I consider he would want you to get a nice new dress for Our Sheena's marriage to Abrach.'

Flora's face was becoming more and more like Cruachan's. 'It's right enough, what ye say,' she said. 'Grampa wouldna have wanted to go to his Maker wi' a bad debt round his neck.' She looked quickly about to see how this statement had been received. Abrach was still immersed in his horrified praying. Our Sheena, it seemed, did not hear or did not care.

'Yes, God would take it out of Grampa for owing us money,' Cruachan said. 'It's really lucky for Grampa we thought of that.'

Abrach's voice wailed across the room. 'O Cruachan, is there no reverence even for the dead, the dead that's your own flesh an' blood, forbye? Help me lift auld Grampa ben here an' lay him in this coffin that he loved.'

As if he was certain that this call could not go unheeded, Abrach started to walk towards the door of the back room. But Cruachan did not follow him. He did not even look at the bent figure of the missionary and it seemed that he had not heard him speak. 'By Hell, there is another thing I just remembered, as well!' he said excitedly. 'Old Grampa, the good man that he was, was right keen that Abrach should have a good new hat. "It is not right for a man on the right hand of the Lord, like Abrach is, going about in a bally hat that is more green than black," Grampa said. "It is a crime that the Ambassador of our Maker should be stumping about this island in a hat stained with dung and dropped on by seagulls." That is what Grampa said to me, God bless him.' Cruachan bent down and breathed heavily on one of the brass legs of the coffin. 'If Grampa had only of known the worth of this good oak coffin

146

I consider he would have sent me over to Oban on the first boat to Matheson with it long ago. "Cruachan," Grampa would have said, "get you on the bally mail-boat with this coffin and sell it to Matheson in the funeral shop and when you gets the money go right into Fraser's next door and buy one of them fine black hats with the fancy silk bands round them like all the swell ministers wear. I wants to give that hat to Abrach for all the praying and interceding he has done for us in the tin house. I don't need this coffin, anyway. The sea is good enough for me." '

Flora was staring down at her sack skirt and smiling as if she was thinking of something splendid.

Abrach walked across the room. He looked as if he was seeing a distant scene of terrible temptation. 'Oh, I know the hat Grampa was meaning, all right, Cruachan,' he said. 'It's no' in Fraser's, though. It's Grant's. Right-hand side o' the window.' He stopped for a moment, as if blinking something out of his sight. 'But ye maun know I couldna accept it. I was lookin' at it just afore I left Oban, for it's true, as Grampa said, I need a new hat right bad. But I tell ye, Cruachan, I couldna stand it if ye bought me a new hat from the proceeds o' that coffin.'

Cruachan did not speak. He rubbed at the coffin and remained silent. What he was waiting for did not take long.

'Whatna problem,' Abrach moaned, covering his face with tense, white hands. 'It would need the widom o' a Solomon. But whatever way I think on dealing wi' it, I just canna bring maself to interfere wi' the wishes o' the dead. The Lord wouldna approve of that. I'll just have to leave it to you to carry out whatever ye say Grampa's wishes were.' He looked up, as if seeing light. 'That's it, Cruachan. It seems I'll just have to take that hat after all. It maun be the will o' God.'

For a long time there was silence. Cruachan did not move from the place where he was standing. It was Abrach who at last led the way to the back room. They covered Grampa with a tarpaulin and carried him out of the tin house and across the grass with bowed heads and short, stiff steps, giving him at least the semblance of grief. They walked past the narrow, water-filled trenches that Grampa had made during his long and unsuccessful search for a dry grave.

'There is no bally sense putting Grampa down any of these holes he dug,' Cruachan said, gasping from the weight of the still form. 'They are wet as the sea and dirty forbye. Besides, we would have to fill them in. Grampa would prefer the waves. The sea will cover Grampa up nice as anything.'

When they reached the old burial place they lashed two heavy rocks to the tarpaulin. Then Cruachan stood as if waiting. He kept looking at Abrach. 'Why doesn't you say a prayer now, Abrach, and let us get Grampa away?' he said.

Abrach shook his head. 'Ye maun know it isna possible, Cruachan. There's no provision in our religion that allows of praying for sinners that desecrate the Sabbath. Neither me or the Lord stands for what Grampa did. Grampa was a horrible abomination in the eyes o' God.'

Cruachan turned to Our Sheena, but before he could speak she shook her head.

'It's just like Abrach tells you, Daddy,' she said. 'There is no prayers good holy people like us can say for wicked Sabbath-breakers like Grampa was.'

Cruachan looked down at the black bundle lying on the wet rocks. 'It just doesna seem right to me, at all,' he said. 'You would think there was some way of seeing off even a big sinner like Grampa. I consider I am just not made to let him go without a word or two.'

He shuffled his feet with slow, awkward movements and then knelt down hesitantly on the wet rocks. 'This man all wrapped up here on the rocks, God, is my daddy,' he said. 'Abrach and Our Sheena say he was a wicked, sinful man and as holy missionaries they certainly knows best. Abrach and Our Sheena say Grampa is a horrible abomination, but maybe there is a small piece of Heaven somewhere beside You even for abominations like my daddy. I certainly hope so, anyway, for I think I am bally near an abomination myself sometimes. Amen.'

He rose stiffly. He took an end of the tarpaulin and, although the missionary was frowning at being compelled to listen to a prayer so coarse, he helped him throw the bundle over the rocks into the sea. A slow spray rose upwards as Grampa, who had dreaded this moment so much, hit the water.

Cruachan continued to look down from the rocks even after the bubbles had stopped coming up. Never had the sea looked so big. He wondered where, in its vast stretches, the body of his father would finally rest. It seemed possible that Grampa might travel a long way. Much farther than he had ever travelled in his lifetime.

18

FLORA looked furtively about the room. Abrach turned away. Cruachan and Our Sheena, who knew the ludicrous routine, became suddenly interested in the fire. Only then did Flora cross the floor and, with a mistrustful backward glance, take from under her pillow on the bed the cracked and tattered handbag in which she kept various family papers, most of them concerned in some way with death or debt.

The handbag and its hiding place were the only private things in the tin house. Everyone knew about them, but not even Cruachan at his most audacious had ever had the temerity to intrude or pry. Under Flora's pillow was a place beyond the veil of the temple.

From the bag Flora took a half-crown, a threepenny and a halfpenny. With another glance over her shoulder, she pushed the handbag back in its place and then, trying to look as if her absence had been without significance and certainly in no way related to the bed, she sat down again.

After a few moments she held the money out to Cruachan as if it had been in her hand all day. 'That's every penny I have,' she said. 'Here'—she thrust it at him—'take it. How much have ye now?'

Cruachan made a quick calculation. 'Six-and-tenpence,' he said. 'That is all I has still—six shillings and tenpence.' He shook his head sadly. 'They is still not going to take me to Oban on the bally mail-boat for that. By Hell, it is a robbery the money they want for a wee short journey like that!'

For a week Cruachan had been preparing himself for the journey to Oban to sell Grampa's coffin. Since the day he had thrown his father's body into the sea he had been unable to look at the long shining box without guilt. Several times he had seriously considered chopping it up. This violent act of atonement had so appealed to him that once he had actually stood over the coffin clutching the axe. But at last, by suddenly remembering various things that Grampa had never said, he had beaten down his conscience and was now prepared to sail to Oban next day—if only he could find the money. A single-journey ticket cost nine shillings and sixpence and even Cruachan could not delude himself into believing that the fare would be suddenly reduced next morning. His plan was to cross to Oban, sell the coffin and do his shopping. Since the mail-boat sailed only once a week, he would get a Macbrayne's steamer to the island of Maree next morning and complete his journey home from there by ferry-boat.

'The dear Lord knows, this is some problem,' he muttered.

No one spoke.

'If I had the time I'd get that old boat of mine painted up and sail myself over there and to Hell with them mail-boat robbers,' he said.

Flora, having bankrupted herself, sat silent. Abrach was so withdrawn in the queer quietness that had come on him in recent days that he seemed unaware of Cruachan's predicament.

It was Our Sheena who spoke. 'I've got some money saved up from my praying collections,' she said dreamily, 'and I has also just received a message from the dear Lord that I should proceed to Oban. You can come with me tomorrow.'

Having made this pronouncement, she leaned back complacently in her chair. Since her betrothal to Abrach a serenity had settled on her face, softening the strong lines and making them almost beautiful.

Cruachan looked at her sharply. 'How much money you got, Our Sheena?'

'A pound.'

'By Goddy, that certainly would take you and me there, all right!' he said excitedly. Then he looked at her with suspicion. 'What's this message you has received, though?'

'Aye! What, indeed? That's what I want to ken as well,' Flora said. 'The last transaction that yin had wi' the Lord landed her in a real pickle o' bother.' She turned sarcastically on the girl. 'Are ye sure there's no' a wee angel wi' a hand in this, too?'

Our Sheena ignored her mother. 'It is not for me to question the wishes of the Lord,' she said gently. ' "Whither He commandeth, I goeth." That is one of the sacred vows I took with the Assembly before I was ordained a holy missionary. Now I know the Lord wants me to be in Oban. Maybe it is just to help Daddy over there. The ways of our Saviour is mysterious. Maybe'—she looked demurely across at Abrach—'it is about the white dress for my wedding. Maybe it is that the Lord has some souls of the wicked for me to save for Him over there.'

Abrach had emerged from his dream, his eyes bright with interest. 'A true servant o' the Lord never hesitates when he hears the voice that speaks within,' he said.

Our Sheena leaned over and placed a tender hand on the missionary's arm. She seemed blind to the discomfort that this obviously caused him. 'I knew you wouldn't mind me going to Oban for a day, beloved, when the dear Lord wants me to,' she said, her hand moving over his.

Abrach looked away. 'Woe to the man that dare interfere wi' the blessed ordinances o' the Lord,' he said uncomfortably. 'Ye'd better haste to Oban wi' all the speed at your command. "Whither He commandeth, I goeth." '

Our Sheena had hoped that Abrach might show some sorrow at losing her even for a day. His face, however, was touched by an emotion more positive than that. What it was Our Sheena did not know, but she felt that it must be pride at her selection.

As they carried the coffin along the track next morning the water gleamed cool and calm beside them. The spring had been dry. But Cruachan knew that it would not last. He hoped that Roddy would be home and that they would have the lazybed made before the rain came. When the mail-boat sailed in, Cruachan splashed out to meet it in his anxiety to see if Roddy were on board. But apart from the helmsman, more raw and battered-looking than ever, and a few boxes of provisions, the boat was empty.

Cruachan and Our Sheena sat themselves side by side in the stern, facing the white sun, the coffin balanced carefully over their knees. There were only four other passengers: young island people returning to their jobs on the mainland after visits home. Cruachan dangled his hands in the water and watched with pleasure the wash that they made. Our Sheena sat very straight, her bonnet tied under her chin and the black silk ribbon fluttering gently about her firm white neck.

When the boatman slipped his jingling leather bag over his shoulder, indicating that he was now operating in the capacity of purser and wanted their fares, Our Sheena opened her purse and handed him the pound.

'Two single tickets, please,' she said, eyeing his beery face with compassion.

The boatman crackled the note. 'You'll need more than this to get ye to Oban, Our Sheena.'

The girl looked at him in the way that she looked at all sinners. She remembered that she had once seen him lurching happily from a pub in Oban. She sniffed cautiously, trying to discern the tell-tale fumes that would account for his silly statement about the fares. Drink was the only explanation that occurred to her.

'The fare is nine shillings and sixpence each,' she said. 'There is more than enough there.'

'That's for only you and Cruachan, but nothing about this coffin. The freight on that coffin's another fourteen shillin's. Coffins is more than people.'

There were no scriptural grounds on which Our Sheena could challenge this. She looked into her empty purse. She did not know what to say and was about to pray for guidance when Cruachan brought his wet palm down on the coffin with a slap.

'By Hell,' he said, 'there is no fare on this at all! This is personal luggage, so it is, and the dear Lord Himself would tell you that. I has been on these boats before, all right, and I know they doesn't charge you any fare at all if you just say: "Personal luggage." ' He nodded his head up and down to emphasize the extent to which he understood the rules.

The boatman stared doubtfully at the coffin. 'If it's personal luggage what's inside it?' he asked, rubbing his head. 'I canna think of anything that a man could cart around in a coffin except the usual thing, and it canna be that . . . can it?'

'Don't you go worrying your head about what's inside,' Our Sheena said severely. 'That is just no business of yours, at all.'

The boatman shrugged and reached out for the fares of the other passengers. He was still mumbling to himself when they reached Oban.

At the top of the concrete steps, leading to the quay wall, the usual scattering of idlers stood, their arms spread over the rail. When they saw Our Sheena and the coffin they made sounds of delight. Here was something of note, something that made all the hard hours of rail-hanging worth while.

Cruachan had not seen so many people for years and the peering faces and the bustle of harbour work beyond made him nervous. Our Sheena, who normally took crowds and staring people as her due, was trying to do two things at once: look about a foot smaller than she was and appear as if every day, all over the civilized world, hordes of people came off mail-boats carrying home-made coffins.

As they went up the steps, a gust of wind swept her bonnet backwards, and because she thought it improper for a woman—especially a missionary—to have her head uncovered in public she let go of the coffin with one hand to clutch at it.

Cruachan was on a lower step and the extra weight coming without warning toppled him backwards. He slithered down the steps with the coffin clattering after him. On the jetty he rolled to a stop, bruised and breathless, but safe. Not the coffin. It shot smoothly along the slipway of moss, over the edge and into the sea.

Up on the quay the people hanging over the rail sniggered and nudged one another. It was a quiet town—still slumbering in off-season calm—and they were not often lucky enough to get anything as diverting as this.

'And may God watch over all those who sail in her,' shouted one red-faced man as the coffin cut through the water like a new-launched ship.

Our Sheena whirled round viciously. 'What're you laughing for?' she snarled. The man gaped for a second at her terrifying bulk and then backed away.

Cruachan had scrambled to the edge of the jetty and was clawing desperately at the coffin. It had floated so far out that he was able to touch it only with the tips of his demented fingers. 'By Goddy,' he screamed, 'get down here with them long arms, Our Sheena, and save this bally coffin before it sails clear to Hell and Jesus out of here!' In its fall down the steps two legs had been broken from the coffin and these now lay somewhere at the bottom of the bay.

From the jetty Our Sheena jumped to the beach. Up on the quay the crowd cheered. 'Dinna get your feet wet, lassie, or ye'll catch your death of cold,' someone shouted.

'Aye! It's ower early yet for paddling. Come back in the summer-time,' said another.

Our Sheena stopped only to shake her fist, then, hitching her skirt almost to her waist, she stepped into the water and stepped out towards the coffin. At the sight of her long legs there was a renewed outbreak of nudging and whistling.

'It is just like the Frollies Berjerr.'

'The funniest funeral I've ever seen.'

Our Sheena waded outwards on her long white legs until the pull of the water stopped her and she stood, like a cautious and precarious stork, still several yards from the coffin.

'Ye'll be wettin' your drawers if ye don't watch, missus.'

From where he lay on the jetty Cruachan shouted at the hilarious throng. 'By Hell, you'd better stop that laughing! God does not like people laughing at me.'

Our Sheena gestured and grimaced at them, and when this did not stop them she spat. 'I hope the dear Lord burns you all up!' she shouted. 'You're nothing but a horde of stinking abominations! All you people up there has the filthy stain of Satan spread all over you. I can see the putrid marks as plain as plain from down here. On the outside you're all washed and starched up to look like angels in them swell dresses and clean shirts but underneath you're as black as only sin can be. God and me can both see that, so we can.'

Her rage against the people who had dared to laugh at her had driven all thought of the coffin from the girl's mind. She had also forgotten about her skirt and it now floated about her in the water like the leaf of a great black lily, with her the strange flower. Her fierce threats and accusations only incited them to louder laughter.

'By Jesus, you bitches and bastards has no right to laugh at me!' Our Sheena screamed. 'God and me works like one and you're laughing at Him too. I know you rotten, debauched town people and all your sinning. You fornicators up there are so lustful you do nothing but roll it with each other from Monday till Sunday. All you men are filling it up with whisky night and day . . . and'—she paused, dredging through her vast experience for the ultimate in depravity—'and you is so eaten up by the devil you even handles your own little daughters when there is no other women for you to beast it with.'

As she clubbed them with these epic imputations, her mind was clear of any disturbing memory of her own immortal transgressions.

'All you fancy women up there is just as bad,' she yelled. The whole wide panorama of sin lay before her—and she knew every inch of it. 'None of you women has got a piece of purity big enough to pass round between you. I consider the Lord is not going to let any of you live much longer, you're so wicked. You women are so keen on waving it you can hardly keep your clothes on long enough to look in the mirror. One of these days the Lord is sure to come cutting through you all with His terrible sword of justice. The sword of the Lord is sharper than anything else in the whole world and He will cut you down so fast you will be gone to eternal damnation before you can put your clothes on.'

The disturbance that Our Sheena had caused in the water had sent the coffin bobbing nearer the jetty and at last Cruachan grasped one of the bedraggled tassels and pulled it to safety. The watchers raised a ringing cheer. Our Sheena mouthed a last terrible insult at them and climbed back on the jetty beside her father. The coffin had deep gashes on all sides and it stood drunkenly on only two legs. Cruachan rubbed tenderly at it until it was dry and then picked off the loose splinters.

'These wee scratches is a pity, right enough,' he said, 'but it does not matter at all. This is still a fine oak coffin that Grampa made. The inside is good as new and nice as ever.'

19

WHILE Our Sheena wrung the water from her skirt, Cruachan sat with his back against the jetty wall looking across the water to the far mountains of Mull. Sitting thus, he felt not so far from Torrismore and the tin house.

Behind him, over the wall, there was a street with motor-cars, shops, hotels and hurrying people. To his left, fishing-boat winches rattled in the harbour. Farther away on his right there was a pier from which passenger boats with black and red funnels sailed to the Outer Hebrides. Everywhere there was noise and people.

Cruachan did not like the noise or the people and by looking steadfastly ahead across the water to the far mountains of Mull he could imagine that perhaps he was still at home, and that there were no people there.

Cruachan did not like the town. In the town he felt unsafe and far away from God. Cruachan did not believe that God ever went to town. He did not think God would be able to stand the noise of the town in His ears or the hard feel of the town under His feet. He was certain that God was not the sort of man who approved of towns at all. Cruachan did not know much about towns except that neither he nor God liked them.

What Cruachan knew about was the feel of rain dripping down on him through the leaky roof of the tin house as he lay trying to sleep. He knew the comfort of warm stone at his back and the pleasure of wet grass under his bare feet. He knew the smell of every plant and growing thing on the island and the feel of every kind of earth of which the island was made.

Cruachan knew about sea tangle slithering through his numb hands at five o'clock in the morning and mist seeping inside his clothes until his thin body shook and shivered. He knew the scent of bog myrtle after rain and the shock of eager spade meeting hidden rock.

Cruachan knew about all these things, and about the misery and hurt of asking but not receiving; of starting but not arriving; of sowing but not reaping.

These were the things that Cruachan knew about. He did not know much about towns at all. And what he knew he feared. He had never yet met a town man who had not either laughed at him or tried to cheat him in some way. Because of these things he was delaying as long as possible the moment when he must take the coffin up the street to the undertaker's. All day Cruachan could have sat with his back against the jetty wall, looking across the water to the far mountains. In such a position and thus occupied he came near to being at peace—even in the town. He was almost asleep when the voice of Our Sheena recalled him.

'It's time you took that coffin up and sold it to the funeral shop so that we can buy our things and, if the dear Lord is finished with me, get back in the steamer come morning,' she said.

Cruachan could not deny this or think of any reason for delay, and because Our Sheena had spoken in a loud voice close to his ear he could not pretend either that he had not heard her. After a few minutes, therefore, he stood up.

When they reached Matheson's they stood uncertainly for a moment at the black window where, in gilt lettering, it said: *John Matheson, Funeral Director, Embalmer and Carriage Hirer.* Timidly, Cruachan opened the black glass door and they manœuvred the coffin carefully into the gloomy interior. It was so dull inside that for a few moments they could not see, but gradually the bare scene unfolded. In front of them there was a small counter of highly polished wood and beyond this a screen of black draperies hiding the back shop. On a shelf at the side there was a vase of artificial lilies and an assortment of huge sea-shells. Cruachan had never seen such shells. The ones on Torrismore were very small. He thought it must have been a very big island these came from. Silently, they put the coffin on the floor. The inside of the shop was so decorous that it seemed almost improper even to breathe. Cruachan felt larger and clumsier in his boots and rough clothes than he had even on the night of his ordeal at Sir Eric's party at the lodge in Torrismore. Our Sheena had never felt so tall before. She stood with her head tilted forward in case her bonnet touched the white wooden ceiling.

Cruachan cleared his throat and then cringed as the sound crackled through the gloom like a volcanic explosion. When the noise had subsided the black draperies parted and a man came through and stood beside the artificial lilies. His face was almost as white as the wax flowers and he wore a black suit, a white shirt and a black tie. Cruachan had always imagined God wearing grand clothes like these and for a moment he was too startled to answer the man when he said, in a deep, ministerial voice: 'Good day.'

The man waited suspiciously for either Cruachan or Our Sheena to speak. He was accustomed to meeting people in various stages of grief, but he had never seen a couple like this before. He did not approve at all of their poor and bedraggled appearance. The dead, he thought, deserved better than this. In the man's opinion the least that the dead deserved was a clean shirt and combed hair. But as Cruachan began to open his mouth the man cast these thoughts out of his mind and leaned forward with professional sorrow. A sale was a sale. Business was not as good as it once had been and the man considered all these new drugs and things were to blame.

'It is about Grampa's coffin,' Cruachan said, shuffling his feet.

The undertaker nodded comfort at him over the counter. *Plain Scots pine. Hearse and one coach*, he thought.

'Certainly, sir,' he said aloud. 'We will attend to everything.' He coughed and then smiled delicately. 'You will want it as inexpensive as possible, of course. We quite understand. Yes. Yes. We quite understand.'

Cruachan and Our Sheena looked at each other.

'When did Grampa die, and where?' the undertaker asked.

'Grampa died a week ago on Sunday on the track when he rolled off the ledge looking for gulls' eggs,' said Cruachan.

The man looked startled. 'Dear, dear,' he muttered. 'This is most unusual. Died a week ago. Goodness gracious!' He lifted the lid of the polished mahogany counter. 'My dear people, we must not delay another moment. If you will kindly follow me through to our showroom we can pick the casket.'

Cruachan knew now that there was something very wrong. He hung back and looked up at Our Sheena. 'What is a casket?' he asked.

The man smiled bleakly and rustled the black draperies. 'Coffin,' he said. 'If you would just come through now and select one for your father.'

Cruachan recoiled.

'Grampa has his own coffin,' he said. 'Six years he took to make it. We is not for picking a coffin at all. We want to sell you a coffin.' Like a salesman who has kept his best wares to the last, he pointed proudly to the battered box lying in the shadows of the counter. 'We have come over here from the tin house with this fine oak coffin that Grampa made to sell it to you because we know that is what Grampa wanted, though he never remembered to tell us. Then I'm going to buy Flora a dress for Our Sheena's wedding and a hat for Abrach.'

The man looked down at Grampa's coffin. It was clear that in all his years of directing funerals, embalming people and hiring carriages he had never met anything like this. 'We are here, sir, to assist the bereaved by selling them coffins,' he said stiffly. 'Not to buy them.'

'I consider you has to buy them before you can sell them,' Cruachan said with an undaunted smile. 'Grampa made this fine oak coffin all himself, so he did. Six years it took him, with him polishing and rubbing at it near every day.'

He bent and rubbed his hand lavishly over the lid to show its smoothness. An instant later he jumped with a yelp of pain. A splinter of wood from one of the gashes had gone into his hand. While he sucked at his wound the man came round the counter and looked down at the coffin.

'Where'd you get this?' he asked suspiciously.

'Grampa made it,' Cruachan said. 'Now we want to sell it.'

The man was examining the tassels of old rope and the two brass legs. Then he came to the plaque which said: *Gentlemen Lift the Seat*. His white face became red. 'What's this?' he said, glaring at the plaque.

'Poetry,' said Cruachan. 'It is not out the Bible, so we consider it must be poetry.'

The undertaker looked from Cruachan to Our Sheena. 'What kind of stunt's this?' he said.

'This is no stunt at all. We want to sell this good oak coffin of Grampa's quick as thunder and get back to the tin house. How much is this coffin worth, mister?'

Professional interest drew the man reluctantly down to the coffin again. 'Maybe this coffin would have been worth a pound or two before it got all these holes in it,' he said, 'but now it just isn't worth anything as a coffin.' He looked keenly at Cruachan. 'If you like I'll give you five bob for it. That oak wood might be some good for something, sometime.'

Cruachan snorted. 'This good oak coffin Grampa made is worth eight or ten pounds, I consider. Even though there is a small scratch or two, you could soon fix that, so you could.'

'Five shillings.'

Cruachan waved his hands with baffled anger. 'By Jesus, you rich town people always want to cheat us poor crofters! I never met a town man yet that did not want to rob the poor. God does not like the way you rich town people treat the poor and one of them days He will send you all to Hell, so He will.'

Without another word, the man took Cruachan by the arm and started pushing him towards the door. 'I don't want your coffin, mister. I only offered you five bob because I thought you needed the money. All you crofters are the same. I'd rather have monkeys than you people. Monkeys are more human than you crofters.'

With the man pushing and Our Sheena leading him by the arm, Cruachan was put on to the street, still shouting. A second later the coffin came tumbling out through the black door after him. The force of it hitting the hard pavement knocked off another brass leg, which rolled into the gutter.

'By Goddy,' Cruachan spluttered, 'I have never met a town man yet who was for God or the poor!'

There were two other places in town where, after his rage had subsided, Cruachan thought they might be able to sell the coffin and with small boys jeering at them and adults staring after them they carried the coffin first to one and then the other.

At the first a man offered to buy the coffin for firewood and when Cruachan shouted at him he threatened to send for the police. The second man met Cruachan at the door and when he discovered what he wanted barred the way and refused to let him in. After this Cruachan and Our Sheena carried the coffin to a field at the top of a quiet side street and sat down on it miserably. There was no other place they could go and in any case Cruachan swore fiercely that he would have no more dealings with town men.

After they had been sitting for a while Our Sheena opened her purse and emptied the contents on to her lap. The coins had a total value of one shilling and threepence. With what Cruachan dug out of his pockets they had only eight shillings.

'We is not going to get home to the tin house with just this,' Our Sheena said.

Cruachan looked glumly along the street. The hardness and strangeness of it all made him uneasy inside. He wished now that he had buried Grampa in the oak coffin and stayed on the island among the things he knew.

'I doesn't know how we're going to get back to the tin house,' he said. 'The Lord does not seem to be for me any longer. Seems to me sometimes the Lord has it in for me, hard and sure. I just doesn't know what it is, but there certainly is something about us poor people that brings the worst out in the Lord, right enough.'

Our Sheena stood up. The salt-water had shrunk her cheap skirt and it was now several inches shorter than it had been. Her shoes were bleached a dirty grey colour by the water.

'If you will keep that mouth of yours shut tight for a minute I will get peace to pray to the Lord about this situation,' she said. 'The dear Lord will see us back to the tin house somehow if I just let Him know about us being scarce of money and not being able to sell this coffin. Besides, I want to let God know I'm over here. Maybe He hasn't noticed.'

Our Sheena flexed her legs like an acrobat and knelt down in the grass. Cruachan slid on to his knees beside her. After some minutes of silence the girl started to rise.

'That's me all finished for now,' she said, 'and we will be looking out for the money.'

20

CRUACHAN rose stiffly from his knees and sat down again on the coffin. 'By Hell, if I doesn't get some food down inside me soon I don't think I'll ever see the tin house again,' he whimpered.

It was now after four o'clock and they had not eaten since dawn. Carefully they covered the coffin with grass and weeds, climbed over the wire fencing of the field and turned again towards the town. Even without their striking burden Cruachan and Our Sheena had a curiosity value and as they went through the streets people stared or turned hurriedly away. Cruachan returned the stares boldly. He was experiencing now a belief that—although he had failed to sell Grampa's coffin—Roddy, his son, would at any moment step from the crowd and run to him with a delighted cry. This was the town that Roddy had come to with the gold watch and Cruachan was certain that if only he watched carefully enough he was bound to see him.

Halfway along one of the streets Our Sheena stopped and gripped him by the wrist. They were standing outside an Italian ice-cream shop. The window was draped with folds of faded pink crêpe paper in the gritty crevices of which many flies had found a last resting place. In the forefront, among jars of boiled sweets, there was a small printed notice which read: *A. Di Felice. Best Ice Cream in the Highlands. International Award Winner.* Below this another card read: *Hot Peas. 6d. a Plate.*

'Wait here,' Our Sheena said, straightening her bonnet and giving her skirt a tug. 'I'll find out what we can get to eat in here.' A bell rang in the shop as she opened the door and again as she closed it behind her.

'By Hell, that's right clever,' Cruachan muttered. 'Right clever.' Vaguely he wondered if it would be possible to get a bell like that on the door of the big brick house.

The thought of eating cheered him, and with a burst of his old confidence he stopped a man walking along the street. 'Seen anything of my son Roddy Campbell along the street there, mister?' he asked with a smile.

The man looked at Cruachan's disreputable clothes and edged a step backwards. 'Who?' he asked, looking over Cruachan's shoulder. 'Where does he live?'

'Roddy Campbell. He lives at the tin house with me and his mammy.'

'What?'

'Roddy lived at the tin house till he come over the water about a week ago to sell my good gold watch so we could buy some food.'

The man would be detained no longer. He hated tinkers. He edged back, took a quick step sidewards and then walked rapidly away.

'By Hell, these town men is the queerest bally people,' Cruachan muttered. 'A man asks them a question and they act all funny and then run as if they was hit on the end by lightning.'

He took off his cap and rubbed his head and stood pondering the strangeness of town people. As he stood thinking of these things, an elderly woman came up and dropped something into the cap that was in his hand. 'Poor auld soul,' she said, 'I had a brother who was ruined in the big war, too.'

As she walked away, Cruachan looked down into his cap and saw there was a threepenny piece glinting in it. As he stared at it the café door opened with a *ping* and Our Sheena came out.

'Come on,' she said, 'we can get sandwiches and tea in here.'

Cruachan held out the threepenny piece and told Our Sheena about the old woman. 'The ways of the Lord is so bally peculiar we might miss something if we go in here to eat,' he said. 'Maybe this small coin here is the start of Him sending the money we needs.'

Our Sheena pushed at him impatiently. 'You're the stupidest man ever, Daddy, as well as the sinfullest,' she said. 'That is not the way God works at all. God does not work with threepennies at a time. I consider God will let us have that money we need all in big pieces and not go footering about with threepennies.'

The inside of the ice-cream shop was dull and cold. The floor was of terrazo. To the left of the entrance was the counter—long, broad and deeply scored by the pocket-knives of the local urchins. Behind this, with his back to the freezer of ice-cream, stood the short, sad proprietor himself—Alfie Di Felice—or 'Mr. Dehfleece', as he was known to his customers. His shirt-sleeves were rolled to the elbows and his large stomach was covered by a white apron, one end of which flapped round his ankles. Brown wooden benches ran outwards from the other wall, and between these were marble-topped tables. These cold slabs suggested a mortuary with 'Mr. Dehfleece' the mournful attendant.

As Cruachan and Our Sheena squeezed themselves into one of the bench seats a small girl came through the bedraggled curtain that screened the entrance to the back shop. She was carrying a trayload of hot peas for a group of youths who sprawled over a table next to a mechanical piano which was pounding out some ancient melody with tremendous vigour.

Our Sheena ordered cheese sandwiches, biscuits and tea.

The youths at the far end of the shop became increasingly noisy despite 'Mr. Dehfleece's' silent disapproval. Clearly, such horseplay must be tolerated. Not only had these patrons paid for their order but they were further increasing the profits by dropping a coin into the pianola each time it tinkled and gurgled to a stop. If only the profits could be increased enough the pianola could be scrapped and replaced by a juke-box like the café's along the street.

Cruachan watched like a fascinated boy as the drum of perforated paper slowly revolved and the keys went up and down as if played by an invisible musician. 'These Tallies certainly have got all the new-fangled ideas,' he said to Our Sheena.

Now the youths had found a new use for their hot peas. They were flicking them at the defenceless pianola. The lid was open and pea after pea disappeared into the dim, vibrating interior or bounced about on the cascading keys. 'Mr. Dehfleece', who had borne all until now with the restraint of a man who knows that he is there to serve the public in all its moods, could not tolerate this abuse of his historic instrument. With a howl he puffed round the counter, his long apron flapping about his feet and his paunch shaking.

The vandals fled. The breathless proprietor followed them to the door with his arms waving. 'Putta the peas down the pianola, the pianola no' play!' he shouted. 'Where's the profit?' But the pianola, having digested the peas, played on.

When Cruachan and Our Sheena left the shop 'Mr. Dehfleece' was poised over the strings trying to scoop out the mess with a spoon.

The air of the town was scented with a mixture of peat reek, fishing-boats and dried seaweed. Cruachan breathed deeply, like a millionaire leaving a memorable dinner. 'I will say these town people know how to make a great meal,' he said, patting his stomach. 'I never knew before that town people was such good cooks. Next time we're over here in the big town, though, I certainly would like to try some of that Tally's hot peas.'

Our Sheena looked at him disdainfully. 'Hot peas is vulgar,' she said.

Cruachan suggested that they should walk about the streets for a while in case God was looking for them in some other part of the town to give them the money they needed for the boat fare. Our

Sheena agreed. 'Maybe also the Lord will let me know what He wanted me over here in Oban for,' she said. They had hardly started out on their expectant trek when Cruachan stopped and peered into a shop window.

'By Hell!' he said, pointing to a watch lying in a velvet-lined box among a display of second-hand trinkets, cheap Celtic jewellery and ugly souvenirs in tartan. 'Look in there, Our Sheena. That looks like my good gold watch lying in that bally box. That certainly looks like the watch I gave Roddy to sell.' Our Sheena stooped and looked, like a mother pleasing a child. 'It looks better than your watch,' she said. 'Your watch never had a clean face like that.'

'I consider that is my gold watch, just the same, and the dear Lord would agree, too. Roddy has been in there and sold it to that dealer, or I is not Cruachan Campbell from Torrismore.'

He pushed open the door of the shop—which *pinged* like 'Mr. Dehfleece's'—and went inside. A tall thin man with spectacles pushed up on his forehead stood behind the counter. He looked at Cruachan with surprise, and then, pulling his glasses down into position, squinted hurriedly along the counter to see if there was anything valuable lying on it. There was a tray of engagement rings and a display of wristlet watches. Casually, the man moved along behind the counter and pushed the exposed goods behind a display card.

Cruachan felt uncomfortable and for a few moments he stood scraping his boots on the floor and moving his shoulders from one side to the other, unable to think of what he wanted to say. 'That's a right nice gold watch in the window there,' he said at last.

'Yes,' said the dealer.

'That gold watch certainly looks like my good watch from the tin house that I gave to Roddy to sell.'

The man screwed up his face. 'Do you want to buy the watch in the window?'

169

'Oh, no. I don't want to buy that watch at all. I sent my son Roddy over here from the tin house last week to sell my good gold watch and I'd certainly like to know if that's it in the window there.'

The dealer decided that the only way to deal with this odd customer was to humour him. 'What's your son look like, Faither?'

'I consider Roddy looks just like me, near as anything, only a whole heap younger.'

'Aye, well, it was a young fella right enough sold me that watch. Oh, about a year ago. Came from one of the islands, he said.'

Cruachan slapped his hand against his leg and laughed excitedly. 'I knew it. The dear Lord knows my Roddy is a real clever boy and that would be him, sure as night and seaweed. I consider you is maybe just a wee bit mixed up about the time, though, because my boy is only over here about a week or so.' He laughed, almost drunkenly, with the elation that was in him at having come this near to Roddy. He could not understand why the man was eyeing him so peculiarly. 'These town men are the queerest potatoes,' he muttered to himself. Aloud he said: 'Roddy is my favourite child. I knew he would sell that good gold watch of mine, all right.' Then suddenly: 'How much now did you give Roddy for that watch, mister?'

The dealer started moving things about under the counter, closing and locking the lids of glass showcases. He ignored Cruachan's question. He could see now that there was no sale to be made. 'I'm closing the shop, Faither,' he said. 'You're keeping me late.'

'Well, anyway, I'm right glad to know Roddy managed to sell that watch. Me and his mammy is depending on that money for some good eating and some good-smelling tobacco.' Cruachan stopped with the door of the shop half open. He shook his head good-naturedly and laughed with the air of a student pondering one of the more mystifying but amusing aspects of human nature. 'Fancy you getting mixed up about the time like that, mister. Time certainly is a real funny thing.' The door *pinged* as he went out, leaving the shopkeeper blinking after him.

When he caught up with Our Sheena Cruachan gave her a gleeful slap on the back. 'I told you that was my good gold watch in there, and so it was. The man in there was too bally close to let me know how much he gave Roddy for that watch, but Roddy is a clever boy. Roddy, you bet, did not give that watch away just for shillings.'

He peered up and down the street, which was becoming dark grey with the early spring night, as if he expected to see his son running towards him brandishing a handful of notes. He laughed again and gave Our Sheena another thump on the back. 'You know what that bally dealer said? That bally dealer, he said Roddy was in that shop about a year ago. Fancy that, and Roddy only over here since the other day.'

Cruachan was laughing so much at the thought of the smart town dealer getting confused about the time that people walking along the street laughed too, although they did not know what they were laughing at. When Cruachan stopped laughing he found Our Sheena staring at him with contempt.

'Them old Greek people was right,' she said, 'them that the Lord has got it in for He first makes mad, right enough.' She shook her head pityingly. 'Roddy is not around here buying you them messages. You is never going to see Roddy again. Roddy had offed with the money from that watch and spent it by this time rolling naked in sin.'

'By Hell,' Cruachan said, 'you shouldn't go saying things like that about your only brother, Our Sheena! Don't you say that again.'

For several hours they wandered slowly about the hard streets of the town. They walked along the harbour, the pier and the promenade. They climbed the hill that dominates Oban and there was so much light in the night sky that when they gazed across the still sea they could see the hills of Morven and the white lighthouse at the entrance to the Sound of Mull. They looked at the engines in the railway station and at the boats in the harbour. They looked at the buses in front of the station and at a tinker family pushing a pram loaded with two children, a set of bagpipes and a collection of pots and pans. But nowhere did they encounter Roddy or receive the money that Our Sheena had said God would provide.

'It looks as if the Lord just did not hear that request you made to Him,' Cruachan said wearily. 'I think maybe you'd better pray a bit more.'

'Oh, Daddy, you is nothing but what Abrach would call a contemptible doubter,' Our Sheena said. 'The Lord will provide that money right enough, but only if we has faith. All us workers in the vineyard knows that. The Lord is never a one for saying no if you has faith and asks Him in a nice holy way, like Abrach and me does.'

They were sitting together on a wall above the sea. Across the road men in blue suits, fishing jerseys and cloth caps were coming from a public house where the closing bell was ringing and a man in a dirty white apron was standing by the door shouting: 'Time, gentlemen, please. Come along now, lads.'

Our Sheena turned disgustedly to her father. 'Them men over there is just full of the devil,' she said. 'Them men is so full of drink and the devil that there is no room inside them at all for the Lord. They must be terrible miserable.'

The men were laughing and talking loudly and seemed to be enjoying life in a way that the sober people who passed were not.

'Them men must be full up with misery at not having the Lord inside them,' Our Sheena said, ignoring the signs to the contrary. 'What they need is saved. They need to have their need for the Lord brought to their attention.' She turned earnestly to her father. 'This must be what the dear Lord brought me over here to Oban to see.'

She waited a few more minutes in tense silence and then rose like one called to a great deed. Cruachan stared after her with respectful eyes.

The fishermen who had been in the bar were now standing about on the harbour or sitting on empty fish-boxes or coils of rope. From his seat on the wall, Cruachan watched Our Sheena move among them, the yellow of her hair gleaming softly in the light of the harbour lamps. He pulled the damp sea air down into his lungs with a deep breath of pride. He knew that his daughter was on God's business. He saw her go up to a man who was standing alone and take his hand between hers. For a few minutes they stood talking. Then the man looked furtively about him and started to walk with Our Sheena towards a cluster of creosoted wooden huts which were used in daytime by fish salesmen and fishing-boat owners. With a backward glance they disappeared behind them. Cruachan was not surprised, for he knew that his daughter liked to be alone when she was saving a man.

It was not long before the man reappeared alone from the shadows. He walked along the harbour and spoke to another man nearby. The second man looked surprised at what he was being told, but after glancing about him in a surreptitious manner he walked across to the huts and vanished hesitantly into the darkness behind them.

Cruachan shivered and turned up the collar of his jacket against the small, keen breeze that was rising from the sea. After a few more minutes he swung himself down stiffly from his seat on the wall. His legs almost collapsed under him with lack of circulation. He stood unsteadily till the blood came tingling back, then he walked slowly up the street, looking into the bright shop windows as he went. The exercise warmed him and as he returned to his seat on the wall the second man emerged from behind the huts and rejoined his companion, who had been leaning against a lamp-post, waiting. They walked along the harbour, laughing. Cruachan saw them stop and say something to a fisherman who was sitting on a bollard with his feet resting on a fish-box. As they departed, still laughing and passing within a few feet of Cruachan, one was saying to the other: 'It's the first time I've had a hymn thrown in as well.'

The fisherman on the bollard seemed to be resisting whatever information had been passed to him. He kept looking uneasily towards the huts and then after the two retreating figures. He pushed his fingers up under the back rim of his cap and scratched his head. Then he put his pipe firmly in his mouth and turned round on the bollard with his back to the huts. But after only a few seconds in this position he turned again, as if drawn to the huts by a force which he could not subdue. Slowly he rose to his feet, and then, looking casually to one side and then to the other, he put his hands in his pockets and strolled across the harbour and into the blackness.

By the time another four men had made the pilgrimage Cruachan was almost insensible with cold and tiredness. He did not mind waiting while Our Sheena saved one or two men, but it seemed likely now that she would be behind the huts for several more hours yet. As far as Cruachan could see, the savings were likely to go on for a long time. Every fisherman in the area seemed to have heard that salvation was at hand. Several had lined up against the rail of a slipway and were patiently waiting their turn to go behind the huts. Cruachan had never seen men so anxious to be saved. One man was reading a newspaper as he waited. Another was slicing thin shavings from a piece of wood. A third was chewing reflectively on a cut of tobacco. It seemed to Cruachan that if he did not do something about getting Our Sheena out from behind the huts he might have to sit on the wall for the whole night.

He stumbled coldly towards the harbour and the maze of huts

and peered behind the first one he came to. It was so black that he could not see anything. He stood very still and listened, but he could not hear anything either. Cruachan hesitated before going any farther. He knew that Our Sheena did not like to be disturbed when she was saving a man, but he was determined that he was not going to spend the entire night sitting on the harbour wall.

He took a box of matches from his pocket and lit one and then moved cautiously, like an intruder in a church, along the narrow lanes between the huts. Just as the match burned his fingers he heard the unmistakable sound of Our Sheena humming a hymn-tune. His heart was thumping as he took another match from the box. As it flared into life, a man came from behind the hut that seemed to be the source of the low but rousing melody that Cruachan recognized as coming from the hymn-book of the Assembly with God as Father and the Holy Scriptures as Law.

'Round the next corner on the right, auld yin, and mind your feet on the nets,' the man said to Cruachan.

When Cruachan stepped to the indicated spot two hands descended on his shoulders and he found himself being held close against his daughter's massive frame. 'By Hell, Our Sheena,' he shrieked, struggling to free himself, 'this is your daddy!'

Our Sheena was so surprised that she could not speak.

'What the Hell is you doing round here all this time?' Cruachan asked, his voice harsh with embarrassment. 'The dear Lord likes saving, right enough, but he does not mean for it to go on the whole bally night, like you're going.'

'Don't go shouting at me like that, Daddy,' Our Sheena said. 'The dear Lord has done what I said He would. Before you go shouting look at this that I've got. Go on,' she urged, 'light another match.'

In the spluttering flame Cruachan saw Our Sheena's bonnet, and in the bonnet a mound of money—coppers, silver and even one ten-shilling note.

'By Jesus, girl, where did you get this?' he gasped, looking about him in the dark as if a crime had been committed there.

Our Sheena giggled at his astonishment, delighted to be in control of the situation again. 'You is just the stupidest man ever, Daddy. This is the money we prayed to the dear Lord to send, and He has sent it.'

'But where? Where did you get it?'

'From them fishermen, of course. The Lord sent it to me through them sinners. Those men were right appreciative of what I done for them. They liked me singing and praying for them and saving them from their abominable ways, so they did, and the Lord made them give me this money.' Our Sheena giggled again at the recollection. 'And so everything has come to pass,' she said. 'The men the Lord sent me over here to save has been saved and we has also got enough money for the fare home tomorrow.'

Cruachan struck another match and put a shaking hand into the bonnet and touched the money that was lying in it. He could see that it was unquestionably real and that there was enough to get them on the steamer to Maree and then on the ferry-boat to Torrismore.

'Fancy that now,' he said in a low voice. 'Imagine the dear Lord sending you that money in behind these old huts. All over the town you and I went, Our Sheena, awaiting for the Lord to give us that money you asked Him for and here it was behind these huts, he meant you to get it all the time.'

Our Sheena nudged him. 'Here, Daddy, is there any more of them fishermen out there still? I consider the Lord might be wanting me to do a bit more saving yet.'

Cruachan grasped her fiercely by the wrist and started to pull her out from behind the huts. 'By Hell, I think you has done enough saving for one bally night!' he said. 'I want to get some bally sleep. This town has made me very tired, so it has.'

He yawned as they walked out of the harbour, but Our Sheena, holding herself very straight, and with her bonnet set precisely upon her head, hummed cheerfully all the way back to the field where they had left the coffin. There they lay down, one on either side of the battered box. Our Sheena kept her bonnet on. She pulled her shrunken skirt down as far as it would go, clasped her hands together and went immediately to sleep.

21

FLORA saw the ferry-boat when it was still several miles out in the water. She had been waiting for it and thinking of it since early morning, although she knew well enough that there was no possible way of Cruachan and Our Sheena getting back until late afternoon.

The house felt damper, colder, quieter and emptier than Flora had ever known it. Often, in moments of anger, she had visualized a lovely life in which she lived gloriously alone. Now, after only twenty-four hours of peace and quiet, she was lonelier than she would have thought it possible to be. With no one to glower at, to question, to harry; with no one to smoulder over or resent; with all presence, and therefore all provocation, removed, Flora was lost. Although the main emotions that Cruachan and Our Sheena aroused in her were contempt and anger, she needed them as other people needed their objects of love, admiration and respect.

As soon as she saw the dark shape on the water coming from the direction of Maree, Flora snatched up her shawl, wound it about her, swung the black cauldron of simmering water from above the fire and hurried out of the house. She wanted to be on the beach when the boat arrived. Stiffly she started to run. Her laces were old and broken and as she ran her boots flapped loosely up and down. In the first fifty yards she tripped and fell on the track. Several times the string round her waist became loose and the sack skirt slid down and wrapped itself round her bony legs, throwing her to the ground again and again. As she flapped and stumbled round the bay, her heart beat in a jumpy way that she could feel in her throat. Her mouth remained open as she gasped air down into her lungs. Despite the protestings of her body, Flora forced herself on. Never before had she been so eager to meet Cruachan. As the boat cut smoothly towards the jetty, she waded out to it with long, awkward strides. So blindly eager was she to get to it that the helmsman had to give the rudder a violent pull to keep from ramming her.

Heedless of the man's outraged expression, Flora grasped the side of the boat and looked in eagerly at Cruachan and Our Sheena. 'Where is it?' she gasped.

Cruachan could not think why she was there. Her excitement worried him. He preferred her normal apathy. He squirmed on the bench seat and looked at Our Sheena, but the girl was looking past her mother to the island. She was scanning the beach and the whole length of the bay, right back to the tin house, like a hungry hawk.

'Where is it?' Flora asked again, trying to see farther into the boat.

Cruachan faced half away, looking at Flora only out of the sides of his eyes. 'Where is what?'

'It. The dress.'

Cruachan stared stupidly. Even now he could not think what she was talking about.

'The dress ye were gettin' me. Where is it? And what else did ye get wi' the money? Have ye any tobacco?'

Cruachan dangled his hand over the side of the boat and swished it limply in the water, filled now with the memory of his promise.

'There is no dress,' he mumbled at last. Silence. 'Don't look at me like that, with them bally eyes, Flora.' He was almost whimpering. 'By Jesus, me and Our Sheena has had an awful time! Them smart town men over there tried to cheat us like they always do to us poor people. God is not in them town men at all, I'm sure.'

Flora stood quite still in the water with the sack floating about her knees. Her hands slid from the boat and fell to her sides where they hung slightly curled. She did not say anything. She remembered that Cruachan had been disappointing her for almost forty years now, failing her as God and the land had been failing him. She could not think why she had imagined that this time Cruachan would do what he had said he would do. Thirty years ago, even twenty years ago, she might have cried. Now her face was impassive. But inside, in the private place that had become her true home, another light went out.

She pulled her broken-off clay pipe from somewhere in the folds of sacking. 'Have ye any tobacco, then?'

Cruachan's dangling hand swirled in the water a few more times. He shook his head.

Flora looked at her empty pipe and then put it back where she kept it. As she waded towards the shore he shouted after her:

'All them town men can think of is cheating us poor people. By Hell, if only they was honest over there that dress I meant to get would be lying right here in the boat!' He waved his arms at her dejected back. 'Hell, Flora, I even saw the dress I'd have got you. It was black, with a belt and kind of bally glass buttons and fancy bows and things.' He searched his memory for any other fashionable details that he could recall from any of the dresses that he had ever seen in the shiny magazines that sometimes found their way from the lodge into the homes of the crofters.

His memory failed and he turned to Our Sheena. 'Tell your mammy what them town men were like and how they tried to get that coffin of Grampa's for just no money at all,' he said. 'Tell her how we had to throw it in the sea.'

The girl ignored him. She was still standing in the bow of the boat like a figurehead, her expression carved of hope, dismay and fear.

As Flora moved slowly up the pebble beach, the sea-water gurgled and bubbled inside her loose boots and squirted out of the lace-holes in small jets. Behind her, Crauchan clambered from the boat. He sniffed at the air and listened to the bracken rustling on the slopes beyond the pebbles. 'Once I get that lazybed done I'll get you a new dress, Flora, don't you worry,' he shouted. 'Taters was bringing thirty pound a ton last year and sure as God it is going to be the same this time.'

He led them along the track, lifting pebbles and weighing them delicately in his palm as if they were gold, picking up shreds of dry seaweed and chewing at them with mysterious pleasure. 'By Goddy, I'll stay on here if I'm the last man left!' he shouted over his shoulder. 'This is the hometown of all us Campbells, every bally one of us. This is where the Lord means us to be. I know, sure as anything.'

Our Sheena had been silent since her arrival. Now, with the tin house only a few hundred yards away, she began to hurry towards it. She was at the door when they arrived. 'Where is Abrach?' she asked Flora in a hard voice. 'Abrach said he would be waiting for me here when I got back.'

Cruachan did not stop. He walked past the house and sat down with his back against the dry-stone wall, like a man going into his favourite chair. Flora tried to get into the house. She wanted to go and sit down where she would not see Cruachan. But at the doorway Our Sheena seized her by the shoulders and pulled her round so savagely that she almost fell. 'I asked you where's Abrach. Tell me where Abrach is.'

Flora tried to struggle free. All the desperate resentment that was in her suddenly gushed up like poison. 'Let me go,' she snarled. 'Get your hands off me, ye big bitch!'

Our Sheena held her firm. 'Answer me! D'you hear? Answer me! Where's Abrach? I've been through the house. He said he'd be here.' She shook her mother viciously, banging her against the doorpost until she screamed.

'He's away!' Flora shrieked, her face twitching with pain but also pleasure. 'Abrach's gone.'

For an instant it seemed that the girl would snap the frail body in two. 'Gone? Where's he gone? Is he praying for somebody? Tell me where he's gone or I'll kill you.' Her voice was terrifyingly low now.

Flora was staring at her through the pain with the triumph of a martyr. 'He's away and ye'll never lay eyes on him again, ye big bitch. He's away on Sir Eric's boat when it went ower to Oban last night. Ye like enough just passed him by.' She laughed hysterically. 'Ye flung yerself at him like a big hoor, but ye couldna keep him. Ye'll have to make do now for your dirty fun wi' the Lord and that angel that did for ye the last time.'

Our Sheena's hands slid limply from around her mother's neck. 'What did Abrach say?' she asked. 'What is Abrach away to Oban for on Sir Eric's boat? Abrach said he'd wait for me here. Is Abrach gone to Oban to pray for somebody?'

'No! He's not away to pray for anybody. Do ye not ken what words mean? Abrach's jilted ye. He's left ye sitting on your big arse, that's what he's done.' Flora was shaking like an idiot.

Our Sheena was stooped towards her now. 'What did Abrach say?' She spoke with almost childish pleading.

'Oh, he said plenty,' Flora sneered, crouching away from the girl as if at any moment she expected another attack. 'He said ye were nothing but a harlot. He cried ye the harlot o' all the ages.'

Suddenly it was Flora who was pushing herself at Our Sheena. 'What's that ye're saying? 'Speak up now, ye're not usually such a dooley wi' the words.'

'When is Abrach coming back for our wedding?'

A cry of glee burst from Flora.

'Ho, ho, ho! Never! That's what I'm telling ye. Abrach's not wanting to get married to a strumpet. Ye couldna blame the man, could ye? Aye! That's what he said ye are, a strumpet. He said ye're a Jezebel. He, he! A bloody Jezebel. Abrach said ye're what the Bible warns men about, and he's not coming back. Ever!'

She whirled round and rushed into the house, like a bundle of rags swept away by the wind.

Cruachan, who had been calling for silence from his place against the wall, rose and tottered stiffly across the grass. 'By Goddy, it's well seen I'm back at the tin house,' he muttered as he passed. 'A man can get no bally peace here at all.'

He went into the house to look for something to eat and Our Sheena was left alone on the grass.

22

THIS morning, Cruachan was early on the croft. An owl was still perched on the cracked and shaky gable of the big brick house and in the morning light the sea was grey. There was a smell of peat smoke and dew-wet grass and seaweed. Cruachan breathed deeply of them all. He was convinced as he stood on the grass that this year—before the heather faded—the big brick house would be finished.

He bent and wet his earthy hands in the dew and rubbed them on his gnarled face. The dew was as smooth as a cobweb and fresher than anything else in life that Cruachan knew. Cruachan thought the dew was so good that even God Himself must use it for washing in.

Gradually, through the mist, mild April sunshine began to break. Cruachan crossed the grass and sat down with his back against the dry-stone wall. He had some things to think out. Very soon his head fell forward until his chin was touching the coarse wool of his jersey and anyone watching would have said he was asleep.

In the early evening Murdo Mhor came.

Cruachan eyed him warily. He did not move from where he was standing with his back against the rusty wall of the tin house. Nor did he say anything. He waited for the money-lender to speak. He did not know what was going to be said, but he could tell from the look on Murdo Mhor's face that it was not going to be to his advantage.

For a while Murdo Mhor did not have the breath to say anything, he had been hurrying so much. He pulled a flask from his hip pocket and gulped at the home-made whisky. He did not offer the bottle to Cruachan. 'That Mairi Fiona of yours is just a hoor, the same as Our Sheena,' he said at last in a voice that was both sob and snarl.

Cruachan stepped forward uncertainly. 'What has Mairi Fiona done?'

'Mairi Fiona is run away with that fancy son of McKinnon, Sir Eric's agent!' Murdo Mhor shouted. 'You Campbells are all the same, just hoors and cheats, that's all.'

'By Hell,' Cruachan said, stepping forward another pace, 'don't go calling us Campbells like that! Mairi Fiona does not even know that dolled-up son of McKinnon and the dear Lord knows that. If Mairi Fiona is not at your house then she must just be hiding somewhere. Mairi Fiona always was a funny girl, not like the rest of us Campbells.'

The money-lender waved his fists so ferociously that it seemed he might attack at any moment.

'Mairi Fiona is away for good and all,' he raged. 'Away, can ye not understand? She went away this afternoon with that McKinnon boy on Sir Eric's boat when it was going to Oban for supplies. That boy has been hanging about making faces in the window ever since Mairi Fiona came to my house. Miari Fiona is not coming back to this island at all. She's for staying over there on the mainland with that pimply-faced wee bastard with the sharp-pointed shoes and the wee feather in his hat. Old McKinnon is not going to like that either. I consider you will get no more work to do up there at Sir Eric's lodge now.' Suddenly he leaned forward until his disfigured face was within an inch of Cruachan's. 'And I can tell you something else.' His voice was gloating now. 'Aye! I can tell you something else. You're getting no bricks up on that puffer from me now. You rotten Campbells have cheated me enough.' As he saw the stunned bewilderment appearing on Cruachan's face, his voice rose triumphantly. 'I'm cancelling all them bloody bricks right away, and if I'm too late do you know what they can do with them? Do you know? They can dump them in the sea. They'll lie at the bottom of the sea before you get one of them, Cruachan Campbell.' He stopped with his mouth hanging loosely open.

Cruachan caught the man by the arm with frantic fingers and looked into his face.

'Step over the wall and come on into the tin house for a while, Murdo Mhor,' he whined. 'Don't go talking like that about them bricks. Come on in for just a little while till Flora makes you a cup of tea. Walking round that big bay tires a man out more than any other thing I know.'

He was pulling as he spoke, trying to drag Murdo Mhor over the wall.

'No, I'm for staying on this side of the wall where I am. You Campbells are so wicked it's safer here.' The money-lender started to shrink away as if Cruachan were a leper making some filthy proposition. He was in the grip of a fierce hysteria. For as long as he could remember he had been the driver of hard bargains; the automatic victor in every financial tussle. The more vicious his usury, the more he had rejoiced. Men had fled the island to escape him; others had starved themselves and their families to repay him; his effigy had been burned on the rocks; his name, his shadow and his likeness had been hideously defiled. All these demonstrations of detestation he had accepted as a tribute to his business skill. To have been bested by a crazy crofter and his idiot daughter was an unbearable affront to his pride.

'If there was a drop left in that big hogshead of whisky I gave you I'd have it back, as well,' he blubbered. 'But Jesus knows at least you is getting no bricks now.' Vaguely he knew this was the only vengeance available to him, to remind the swine over and over again that the bricks he wanted so much would never come now.

'Don't go saying that about the bricks, Murdo Mhor,' Cruachan whimpered. He scrambled over the dry-stone wall and tried to get hold of the man's arm again. 'Come on in and have a cup of tea, Mairi Fiona's just a young girl. Don't go worrying about her, Murdo Mhor, or saying what you just said about them bricks.' He was cringing in front of him, like a slave begging for his life. 'You and me can make some other arrangement. Maybe you could take Flora and Our Sheena back round there with you instead. Our Sheena is a brave big heap of girl and she could pray for you as well. Not many men has a woman that can pray for them as well. And Flora would not look too bad if you got her a new dress and some new laces for her boots.'

He would have offered an arm, a leg—even his soul—for the bricks, but at that moment the money-lender leaned forward and sent him sprawling from the wall.

'Cheats and hoors,' he sobbed. His face had turned a heathery colour and there was a white foam in the corners of his mouth. 'That is all you Campbells is, every one and all of you.'

Cruachan lay where he fell with one leg twisted under him. His fingers scrabbled at the grass.

'Maybe you could let me have some of them bricks, then, Murdo Mhor,' he implored. 'Just a few. God would want me to get a small dose of them bricks, sure as night, seeing you did have Mairi Fiona for a little time.'

The money-lender started to moan. 'By Christ, I have not had Mairi Fiona at all! That girl is as slippery as sea-wrack.' His eyes clouded over with bitter memory. 'There is just no way a man can hold her down if she is not for it. I tried everything.' A sigh came from behind his stumpy teeth. 'Everything! But that girl is just a bitch like the rest of you Campbell bastards. I even promised her I'd go to Oban and buy some pink ribbon to tie on that long black hair of hers. But no! No! She was rolling her eyes about and looking at the window and listening like a bat for that fancy

187

McKinnon boy all the time I was telling her about the nice pink ribbon.' Tears were rolling from his eyes now as he thought of how he had been defrauded by the conspiring father and child. 'A hoor. That's all she is. Just like Our Sheena and like Flora was before her, as well.'

Cruachan staggered to his feet, took the nearest stone and hurled it at the money-lender.

'Don't you go calling Flora like that, now!' he shouted, searching for another stone. 'Neither me nor the dear Lord will stand for that. I'm putting up that big brick house over there for God and He does not like people cursing me or mine.'

The first stone hit the money-lender in the stomach, but it did not hurt him much. The second hit his shoulder and rebounded along the side of his face, drawing a thin trickle of blood. He did not wait for any more. He turned and ran along the track until he was beyond the stones that Cruachan hurled after him. Then he turned and pointed at the big brick house. He started to laugh and his words came flying on the wind that had begun to come in from the sea. 'And that thing there, that thing that's for God. Well, He'll have to wait, for not a brick will you get from me.'

When he had gone Cruachan stumbled over to the tin house and slumped down on the step with self-pity flooding up inside him like a burst drain. He was filled with a sense of staggering injustice, of enormous futility. All his life he had been a sinful man. He knew that. But always he had striven in the best way he could to give God the honour that he knew was God's due. God had given him a painful urge to grow things out of the earth and at the same time set him down on earth out of which nothing would grow. Despite this, Cruachan had loved God still. He had loved God when he was hungry and there was nothing to eat; when he needed comfort and there was no comfort.

With all his being Cruachan had loved the island too, and in the best way he knew had tried to live there because he felt that this was what God required of him. A million times he had sunk his spade into the sodden peat and watched the black water ooze up, with despair pressing in on him like death itself.

Year after year he had put down his seed potatoes and sown some oats and always there had been hope inside him, but every year the harvest was so poor that Cruachan had wept. Then, when the spring came again, new hope rose, carrying him on for another year. He had gone on all his life in this fashion not only because he had to try to grow food to live but because he believed that this was what God wanted of him. Cruachan had been weak. The litany of his sin was endless, but in his own way he had always striven to keep faith with God. He had always tried to give God His place and he had believed that if he did this God would be just. He had been filled with such an urge to worship God that without money or skill or encouragement from anyone he had set out to build a big brick house in His honour. He had even, in the end, sold his daughter for a load of bricks so that he might continue with the house when all other ways of continuing it had been denied to him.

Now God had withdrawn the bricks.

Cruachan could not understand it and as he sat on the step of the tin house and looked through the moonlight to the long shadow of The Angels on the beach a terrible bitterness for the heartlessness of his Creator started to burn in his chest. For the first time in his life Cruachan felt like cursing God.

Tears rolled from his exhausted eyes.

God had withdrawn the bricks.

A shudder ran through him and a weird cry burst from his lips. He jumped to his feet and started to run across the darkening, wind-raked croft towards the big brick house. On the threshold he stopped, surveying the broken walls, the sagging lintels, the waist-high weeds, with tormented eyes. For thirty-three years he had slaved, schemed and sinned to bring it this far. Now God had withdrawn the bricks.

He bounded into the shadowy interior and pounded his fists on the ragged walls. The wind seized his cries of pain and whirled them through the vault of the roof to the assembling clouds above. From one end of the house to the other he staggered, kicking the walls, pelting them with rubble, battering them with his shoulders until his body was so sickened that he had to stop. He searched feverishly over the walls for crevices into which he could force his cracked and bleeding fingers in an effort to dislodge the bricks. Here and there the impoverished mortar cracked and he stumbled back in a pall of dust, the masonry crashing on to his feet and against his legs.

God had withdrawn the bricks.

Through his brain the words pounded, flooding him with a terrible need to profane, to violate, to demolish. Like a priest driven mad by some unbearable blow, he craved ways of desecrating the place he had dedicated to God.

He urinated, like a cat defiling the lair of its enemy. Then, his face covered in blood, his body shrouded in dust, he raced over the grass to the small, disintegrating hut that wobbled in the wind behind the tin house. He wrenched open the door and seized the pail. He dragged himself back across the croft. For a moment he swirled the noisome load like a connoisseur and then hurled it over the front turret—the place that had to be God's very own, the very altar of the temple—in a splurge that made him retch and then, as he watched it dribbling down the bricks, guffaw.

'Take that, you big bastard!' he cackled.

He stood for a moment with the rising wind gripping at his jersey and then he fell sobbing into the bracken.

23

SOMETIME during the night Cruachan was wakened by the wind. It was rushing at the house like a demon, lifting loose sections of the tin walls and clanging them down again until the place rang like a smiddy. He lay on his back and listened, too frightened by the din and the deep shuddering of the old house to move. He could feel Flora's tense body beside him, sharing his fear.

For several hours Cruachan had been in a sleep of incredible weariness. His crazed assault on the big brick house had left him almost cataleptic with exhaustion. For ages he had lain in the bracken too afraid to move. Then, at last, he had crept to the house and crawled into bed, ignoring both Flora and Our Sheena as they sat at the fire listening to the mounting thrusts of the wind.

Several times every year the house was buffeted and shaken by storms. In a structure so old it was a fearful experience, an ordeal to which they never became inured. Always the Campbells emerged like castaways of some cosmic upheaval—white-faced, dark-eyed, shocked; astonished to have survived.

As the wind had gathered through the evening, Flora had glanced repeatedly at Our Sheena. Several times she had tried to lure her daughter into some talk that would distract her mind but without avail. The girl seemed unaware of the loud protestings of the roof and walls, immune to the countless draughts which swirled the silken peat ash from the hearth until it hung in the room like a veil. In the week that had passed since Abrach's flight from the island Our Sheena had been suspended in melancholy, eating little, leaving the house only for brief, listless walks as far as the limits of the croft and back. She rose at the same hour as her father and mother every morning and dressed completely in black, as if Abrach were dead. Then she returned to her room and spent the major part of the day lying motionless on the bed, brooding on her second bereavement within months. Apparently there was no comfort to be drawn even from the Bible. It lay open on the floor in a corner of the room, as if it had been thrown there. The barrier of the girl's trance was insurmountable, and Flora, with growing dread of the din, had poured herself a last cup of stewed tea from the pan hissing by the fire and then gone to bed.

The wind was from the west and in the comparative silences that came between gusts the sea could be heard rising and falling thunderously on the pebble beach. Cruachan knew what a rising sea and a wind with west in it meant. He lifted the blankets higher on his face. They were damp from the dripping roof.

'Are ye waken?' Flora's voice was like a frightened child's.

'Yes.'

He heard her sigh and the tenseness of her limbs relax. There was comfort even in a word.

Somewhere water was entering the house in a steady stream.

They lay listening to the rain drumming on the tin roof and to the wild commotion surging round the house, shaking it, tugging at it, striving, it seemed, to lift it from its foundations and carry it away into the distracted night.

Suddenly the outside door was blown violently open, slamming against the wall with a clatter that made Flora scream. Through the opening a terrific blast of wind and spray deluged into the room, almost sweeping the clothes from the bed. Cruachan struggled on to the floor, his feet splashing in the water that had gathered there. He pushed his way through the flying spume and edged the door shut. The wind battered on it, threatening to smash it open again, as he groped about on the floor for the wedge that held it. He swore to himself that next day he would repair the lock. It was the same oath that he took every time the door was blown open. When it was secure again he stood uncertainly in the darkness, sodden as if he had been plunged into the sea. He splashed to the fireplace and lit the lamp, then blinked about the quivering room. Our Sheena was coming through the door, fully dressed. Her face was very white.

'The sooner you get that big brick house finished, the better,' she said. 'It's terrible through there.'

'Aye! And it's terrible through here as well,' Flora whimpered. 'I'm soaking wet. This house will be the death o' us all.'

Cruachan turned away from their accusing eyes and manhandled the old deal table across the floor and jammed it tight against the outside door, which was already bulging above the wedge as if at any moment it would splinter apart. The awful noise of the storm and the booming and rattling of the house filled him with terror. Only a few hours before he had cursed God and profaned His temple. Now he was certain that God was rearing up against him.

Cruachan knew that the rusty walls of the tin house and the rotting beams which held it together could not long withstand the gale that was now coming in from the sea. Several times during the previous winter he had thought the house was being blown down, but tonight the towering wind was coming in with a power that he had never known before. He sat down on the edge of the bed with his feet in the water. There was nothing to be done but sit on the bed and wait.

Flora had stiffened into rigid silence. She lay with the wet bedclothes drawn up over her face so that only her wide, frightened eyes could be seen in the glow of the lamp which, despite the fury all around, burned with steady serenity inside its sheltering glass chimney.

Our Sheena sat on a wooden chair, withdrawn again after the few words she had spoken; unaware, it seemed, of the tumult. She had the manner of a fatalistic traveller whose journey has been interrupted and who is waiting patiently for the arrival of another train.

The wind was lifting the roof at one end and shaking it like a blanket, sending the stunning sound running in a quivering wave the whole length of the house until it seemed that everything must collapse. There was so much rain and spray being deluged down on the metal shell that sometimes it seemed the house must have been swept out to sea. Water flowed and sprayed through the perforated roof and walls in so many places that there was no purpose in trying to catch it or escape it. There was no escape for any of them from the rain, the wind or the terrifying sounds of the old house being smashed and torn apart.

The rocks which hung down the side of the house to keep the roof on were tossed about like pebbles. They struck a sonorous requiem on the walls. In Cruachan's ears they were the hammer-blows of some vengeful messenger of God demanding admittance.

Off the shores of the island the west wind built the sea into big masses of white water which fell on the beach with a sound like heavy gunfire. When the waves exploded, rocks flew through the night like shrapnel. On the stacs to the south-west the sea cracked down on the ragged fangs and shattered into a foaming white tracery. The west wind caught up the flying water and hurled it down on the groaning house with vicious ardour.

The wind and the rain were rushing at the house as if they hated it. They came rushing at it until Cruachan could not believe that anywhere in the world was there any more wind or rain left, but even then the wind and the rain kept on coming. They kept on coming out of the west and off the sea and making for the tin house as if they had been specially sent. They came rushing at the flapping, sagging, squealing carcass of the house with fiendish eagerness until the beams snapped and the rusty metal rended and the roof went soaring over the croft like a bat.

Even then the wind and the rain were not finished. They came rushing and thudding at the Campbells as they ran across the sodden croft to the shelter of the big brick house. Flora was the last to arrive. She arrived, moaning pitifully, holding the sodden sack to her shivering body. She arrived in her bare feet because her boots had been sucked down into the flooded ground halfway across the croft. Cruachan and Our Sheena were already crouching there when the wind blew Flora in. Cruachan's bony frame stuck jaggedly through his wet clothes and he trembled as if ill. Our Sheena stared fixedly ahead as if she did not know or care where she was. Flora squatted down with her back against a wall and her bare feet drawn underneath the sack-skirt.

The storm found them again within seconds. It came screeching in from the heaving sea, where it was made, and battered itself against the cracked and tilted walls of the brick house to get at them. The main front wall behind which the Campbells sheltered received the full weight of the onslaught. The rain waterfalled down the outside of the house and washed away the mud which Cruachan had used instead of cement, and the wind pushed at the brickwork until the frail walls shook.

Inside, Cruachan and Flora and Our Sheena waited and prayed for the storm to weaken, but there was no sign of that yet. Above them, bricks fell from the walls of the roofless shell and objects which they could not see hurtled down around them, smashing on the ground and showering them with hard fragments. So much mortar and rubble tumbled from the darkness above them that

Flora began to weep, and then scream, with each new fall. Cruachan crawled about among the bracken looking for some part of the house that would give them greater shelter, but there was none. Flora's terrified wailing followed him through the bracken. Desperately he fumbled about for something that would shelter them, but there was nothing. The only possible protection would be a section of corrugated sheeting from the tin house. He decided to get one. As he crawled fearfully out of the big brick house, the sky to the east held the first grey tinge of dawn. All night he had hoped that with dawn the storm would stop, but there was no sign of that yet. As he crept across the croft, the wind howled around him, grinding him down to the deluged earth.

When he reached The Angels he could go no farther. He collapsed against the cold whinstone feet and the spray from the white and angry sea fell on him where he lay and the rain ran down the inscrutable faces above him so that it looked as if they wept. He was too exhausted to fight against the wind any more. He could not go on to the wreckage of the tin house. He got to his feet and started to run back to the brick house. The wind caught at his body, lifting him up and carrying him jerkily across the croft like a hopping puppet. Halfway there, he realized that the high front wall behind which Flora and Our Sheena waited was tilting slowly backwards, its surface rent by a multitude of gaping cracks. As he cried out, the wind smashed him to the ground. He lay and watched, like a man seeing his own death.

With a shuddering sound that obliterated even the storm, the front wall fell and the earth shook. The tremors ran through Cruachan's beaten body. The two crow-stepped gables that he had built to save him using scaffolding were the next to fall, quickly followed by the back wall and the stunted spire.

All that remained now was the turret that Cruachan had seen as the very heart of the house, the place that would be sacred to God Himself. It hung for a second in the staggering night, seemingly without support, and then disintegrated as if struck by a gigantic hammer.

Altogether it had not taken more than a few seconds for the big brick house to come down, even though it had taken Cruachan thirty-three years of his life to put it up.

24

I T WAS the first week of May; three weeks after the storm. Cruachan sat on a rock by the Bay of The Angels and looked across the island. Up on the hill a brown-and-white cow was bent to meagre grass. A big bird which he could not recognize swooped from the mysterious shadows of the mountain and flapped out over the glistening sea. It was warm again and the clear green water of the sea rippled in over the white pebbles almost up to his boots. Cruachan was grateful for the sunny spell. The rain had come down almost every day since the storm and would almost certainly continue to come down, with only short intervals of dryness, throughout the rest of the Hebridean summer.

Against the dry-stone wall he had fixed some corrugated sheeting from the tin house into a shelter the shape of a tent. The sections were held together only by rocks leaning against them at the bottom and by their own weight at the top. In the slightest breeze they rattled like the tin house had done and they let in the rain in exactly the same way. When it was dry Crauchan felt quite comfortable and at home in his tin tent, even though he looked like a dog lying in a kennel. His eventual plan for his new home was to hold it together with a spider's web of tarred ropes weighted at the end with rocks, but so far he had not had the time to do this.

Little more than the stone foundations remained to mark where the original tin house had been, with out of them, here and there, a broken beam pointing rottenly to the sky.

The remains of the big brick house already looked to Cruachan like an old and familiar part of the scenery. By the end of the summer the bracken and nettles would have advanced over the ruins and made them part of the island's history.

Flora and Our Sheena were still under the bricks. Cruachan had refused all offers of help to get them out. He did not see that they could be given any fairer resting place.

At the other end of the bay a steamer was anchored. It was the boat that had been sent for the first stage of the island's evacuation. All morning Cruachan had sat on his rock and watched the people go along the track towards the boat, stumbling under the burden of their belongings—the old chairs, the battered chests, the blankets tied to the backs of the women and the men bent under their bulging creels. He had waved and called his farewells, but stubbornly he had refused to accompany them round the bay. Now he realized that the boat was moving. It was too far away for him to recognize the figures that lined the rail, but there came to him, rising and falling as the breeze caught it, the sound of their voices singing. For a few moments he listened and then he rose from the rock and with the water swirling around his boots he began to sing with the drifting voices.

It was the forty-sixth psalm.

'God is our refuge and our strength, in straits a present aid; therefore, although the earth remove, we will not be afraid.'

He went on singing hoarsely until the boat became a speck and they were gone. Gone like Flora; like Our Sheena. Gone like Mairi Fiona and Grampa. By the end of the summer they would all be gone.

He rubbed at his eyes and looked aimlessly about him. For a long time he stood not knowing what to do, then there came to him, drifting over the island, the sweet smell of bog myrtle, new heather shoots and earth. It seemed to give him purpose. He walked up the beach and the pebbles crunched under his boots. He stepped over the dry-stone wall and went slowly through the grass. All around lay the things that had always been there and the new things from the tin house that was gone.

Cruachan resolved that the first day he had the time he would clear them all away.

On the grass lay his spade and his creel. As he looked down on them he was filled with an enormous desire to open the earth and grow something out of it. It was as if all his terrible yearnings were flowing in this single channel now that the big brick house was gone. As he stood on the squelching ground of the croft, he swore that before the burns on the hill reached their late spring level he would have carried the earth for a lazybed and have some potatoes down in the ground.

His face was rich with the haggard tranquillity that comes only to saints and great sinners.

He looked across at The Angels and then, as if he saw there an expression of disbelief, he swore again that sure as anything, sure as high and low water, sure as leaves do fall and men die, before the spring was over he would have dug himself a lazybed.

All he would wait for before starting was the return of his son Roddy to help him.